I0769452

Kemper's House

Kemper's House

By

Frank Saverio

Kemper's House by Frank Saverio

Copyright ©2024 Frank Scalise

All rights reserved. No portion of this book may be reproduced or used in any form without the prior written permission of the copyright owner(s), except for the use of brief quotations in a book review.

Cover Design by Touqeer Designs

Code 4 Press, an imprint of Frank Zafiro, LLC
Redmond, Oregon USA

This is a work of fiction. While real locations may be used to add authenticity to the story, all characters appearing in this book are fictitious. Any resemblance to real persons, living or dead, is purely coincidental.

This work also contains fictional song lyrics, song titles, podcasts, films, and other pop culture references that are wholly fictional and the creation of the author. Any actual celebrities mentioned are referenced in a fictional manner, and should not be construed to have said or done anything in real life that is attributed to them within this work.

ISBN: 978-1-962889-02-5

For Piers Anthony,
who inspired both the reader and the writer in me

*Two possibilities exist: either we are alone in the universe or we are not.
Both are equally terrifying.*

— Arthur C. Clarke,
1917-2008

1

The alarm drew him from his dream.

Baw. Baw. Baw.

He tried to cling to the images, but they slipped away in the ethereal way all his dreams did. Kemper envied those people who said they vividly remembered their dreams. He also wondered if they were, in fact, lying.

The antiseptic odor of the air in his pod was the first thing he sensed after the insistent alarm. He blinked. Even that small action took great effort. He followed it up by deepening his breath, slowly at first, just like he'd been trained. The techs told him cryogenic pod minimized atrophy through electrical stimulation, but nothing replaced actual movement.

Baw. Baw. Baw.

Take it slow, he reminded himself.

Deeper breaths.

More blinking.

Work the jaw back and forth.

Then, slowly, twitch the extremities.

Baw. Baw. Baw.

The process lasted about an hour. Or so he thought, anyway. His perception of time was muddled, partially as a result of coming out of cryo, but also from the mind-bending explanations the scientists gave him regarding time dilation.

How long had he been asleep?

He knew the ship chronometer would have one answer.

But the planet they were approaching—and he hoped it was that planet, because engaging the re-animation protocol for anything else meant something had gone terribly wrong—would have a different concept of how much time had passed.

Ditto for Earth.

As he lay in the pod, slowly increasing the depth of his breathing, now twirling his hands gently at the wrist and flopping his feet from side to side at the ankles, he tried to look past the frosted glass that encased him. The light beyond was dim and the shapes indistinct. This was supposed to ease his transition.

It only made Kemper more anxious.

Baw. Baw. Baw.

Soon the automated process would reach the point of asking if he were ready to disengage the hermetic seal. Pop open the pod and join the atmosphere of the ship at large. Begin the true mission.

He tried to focus on that eventuality.

Tried to prepare.

But one thought clanged in his mind, even louder than the ship's alarm.

Except for the crew of this vessel, everyone I have

ever known has been dead for centuries.

Kemper began to cry.

The psychologist had warned him this might be his reaction. At the time, Kemper had rejected the idea. He had no family and few friends. He was a soldier, an explorer, who had seen terrible events and experienced hard moments. But now that moment with the psychologist made him feel like he'd been a child in the middle of the day in the company of a parent. Now that night had fallen and he was alone in his room, he felt differently.

The act of weeping was understated due to his minimal state of physical wakefulness. A few tears slipped from the corners of his eyes and tracked past his temples to drip into his ears. He focused on the sensation of the liquid drops pooled there on the ledge of cartilage. Then he swallowed languidly and took control of himself.

The alarm continued. Eventually, an inquisitive beep cut through continuous sound and drew his attention to the glass surface in front of him. A query flashed there.

COMPLETE REANIMATION?

Kemper raised his hand slowly and touched the screen where it said YES.

2

When Central asked Kemper to lead the expedition to Kyra-2B, the hardest part about saying yes *wasn't* that he was already retired.

After all, he'd been retired barely a year and military careers were brief. While most of his civilian peers were barely mid-way to their pensions, he was already drawing his at only forty years old.

The idea of a mission wasn't daunting, either. He wasn't that far removed from the intensity of active exploration—and occasional combat. Decades of anticipating such moments made them seem less imposing than they might to those same civilian peers toiling in office jobs.

He'd kept himself in good physical condition, too, out of a lifetime habit. Truthfully, the exercise and martial arts training filled the hours. There wasn't much else to do, he discovered. He still hadn't worked out what his life was going to be now that he'd taken the bars off his collar and exchanged his uniform for nondescript clothing. There was no longer a partner in his life for him to spend his days with. His wife, also an officer, had died in a training accident. Kemper never remarried. Even years later, his duties hadn't allowed for more than a few brief dalliances.

He imagined the lack of family connections had influenced Central's decision to offer him the mission.

It certainly factored into his initial desire to say yes.

One thought held him back—the prospect that he might lose his house.

It was a simple three-bedroom, constructed of treated wood encased by stone. Large, east-facing windows let the light into the main living areas during the morning hours. The open layout meant the early brightness filled most of the house while he drank his coffee and prepared for the admittedly empty day. Despite his lack of purpose, the light seemed to welcome him. It gave him hope.

Intellectually, he knew the house was built solidly enough it could still be standing in fourteen hundred years. That wasn't the problem.

The problem was, it wouldn't be his anymore.

It was that kind of mission.

The Central Space Administration tried to convince him. First, Vasim Gupta, the project head of the CSA, appealed to him on the basis of money.

"All of the crew members will liquidate their assets prior to departure," he told Kemper. "Your resulting net worth will be placed in trust. By the time you return, you will be incredibly wealthy. You can buy any home you like."

Kemper didn't want just *any* home. He wanted *his*

own house. And that meant not selling it now.

Reluctantly, Gupta agreed to modify the mission rules for crew members. Instead of his financial assets being placed in trust, Kemper could opt for the house instead. They promised him his family could act as stewards of the property, living in and maintaining the house while on an irrevocable contract.

"Your home will be waiting for you when you return," Vasim Gupta promised him. "As will the entire world."

However, Kemper's lack of family went beyond his unattached status. "I don't have any family," he explained to the director. "I'm an only child. So were both of my parents."

"That is admirable," Gupta noted, "and responsible."

Kemper knew what he meant. Under the crush of overpopulation, the coalition governments urged families to limit offspring to one child per couple. Kemper himself had gone a step further out of a sense of duty and patriotism—he and Holly had planned to abstain entirely from having children. After her death, the decision became less about patriotism and more about the reality of his existence. Hard to have a child without a partner.

The existential threat of overpopulation had weighed on him, but Kemper wondered if his own experiences had trivialized the concept of extended family. He'd grown up with no experience of any family beyond his own household. It wasn't until he joined the military right out of primary school that any expanded sense of family became clear to him. He marveled at the connections some of his fellow soldiers had to siblings, cousins, aunts and uncles.

This lack of immediate family was only a minor obstacle in the eyes of CSA. Gupta assigned a staff member to do some genealogical work, and that staffer managed to locate multiple distant cousins in Kemper's family tree. Several had been amenable to acting as steward. After a few interviews, Kemper selected a Danish woman named Jensine, and the problem of his house was resolved.

So, Kemper agreed to captain the journey to the Kyran system. He liquidated the remainder of his assets and donated it all to his alma mater, funding a scholarship in the Leadership Studies program. If nothing else, he thought that might be a worthwhile legacy.

Before he left home for the training and preparation center in Texas, he took in one last bright, beautiful morning at his house. He listened to the peculiar silence that every home has while the light flooded the room. Then, he drained the last of his coffee and gathered his personal gear.

As he exited the bedroom, he paused suddenly in the short hallway. On a whim, he dropped his bag and withdrew a coin from his pocket. Years ago, people had used coinage as currency, he knew. That custom ended nearly a century ago, but the practice of minting coins for other ceremonial purposes lingered.

He turned over the metal disc in his fingers. It was a challenge coin from his early days in the service. Those on the spaceflight path were awarded the coin when they completed the initial phase of training. Carrying it wasn't a formal regulation but doing so was a strict informal rule. If another spacer challenged him to produce it and he did, the challenger owed the first round of drinks next outing. If the challenged spacer didn't have the coin, the penalty was severe—he would be picking up the tab for meals during the next ten outings. That was unless he later successfully challenged the original challenger and won.

I won't be needing this for a long while, he thought. *Not where I'm going.*

Kemper glanced around, considering. Then he remembered a loose stone on the mantle of the fireplace. He padded over and worked the stone free. That took a few moments, because the stone atop it overlapped, holding it in place. Once he had removed the stone, he used the edge of the coin to gouge out a flat bed in the grout underneath. Then he lay down the coin and replaced the rock, wedging it in tightly.

He gazed down at his handiwork. Since the stewardship contract for the house forbade any construction or remodels—only allowing for repair work—he thought there was at least a chance the coin would be waiting for him when he returned.

Then again, fourteen hundred years was a long time.

The briefings alone went on for two full weeks, feeling more like an extended seminar than preparation for an expedition.

Kemper sat with the rest of the crew, enduring the

early stages of the presentation. Different aspects were handled by their respective experts—astronomers, engineers, physicists, astrobiologists, military tacticians, pilots, and so on.

The crew numbered six, including himself, plus three alternates as a reserve pool, in case someone became sick, injured, or simply unable to perform the mission. The crew members were carefully chosen over the course of nine months and were among the best in their fields while also representing a staggering amount of human diversity in nationality, race, and gender. These variances were purposeful. Gupta stressed that first contact should present not only the best of humanity, but also its breadth. Psychological profiles were matched to the mission and to the other team members.

Kemper knew no selection process was even close to perfect. But he was confident in this crew. His own input weighed heavily in Gupta's ultimate decisions on personnel, which made Kemper feel like this was already closer to being *his* crew.

"The Kyrans," continued Renata Vecchio, the chief cosmic anthropologist making this presentation, "did not intend for their first messages to reach us. Much like our own radio and television waves blasted out from earth in the early to mid-twentieth century, these communications were meant for their own populace. When we received them three years ago, it was essentially as eavesdroppers."

"I thought TV and radio waves dissipated over long distances," said Petry, the engineer.

"They do," Vecchio replied. "These waves did not."

"Why not?"

She pressed her lips together. "I'll leave that for the physicists to discuss."

"Fine," Petry said, biting off the word. "Did we learn anything on these creatures' personality?"

Vecchio paused. "Personality? For a civilization?"

"He means culture," said Ouyang Shu, the mission's cosmic anthropologist.

"He *means*, are they warlike?" Petry corrected.

"Based on the nature of their transmissions, the Kyrans appear more peaceful than our own species," said Vecchio. "As I stated, that conclusion is based on inference, not direct evidence."

Petry frowned. It was clear the engineer did not like unknown variables. It was also clear where Petry stood on the great debate of the day—whether or when humans should travel to the Kyran system and seek out contact. Petry seemed to favor those who saw things through the lens of the potential military threat the Kyrans posed.

Kemper understood not liking unknown variables. He himself had a captain's healthy fear—or at least cautious respect—for the unknown. However, he also recognized, for him, it was fear that provided the spice. Perhaps that was why his greatest concern, despite being a soldier, wasn't whether the Kyrans possessed superior technology or had the drive of a conqueror. His own imperative was more firmly rooted in the existential threat his own people had caused here on this planet— too many people, and dwindling resources.

"Don't you think we should find out—" Petry began.

"Moving on," Vecchio said, speaking over the engineer. "Our physicists have calculated these messages originated on Kyra-2B roughly three hundred years ago. Our civilization analysis team, of which I am a part, estimated the Kyrans' technological level at that time to be the rough equivalent of our own late twentieth century."

"Three hundred years ago," repeated Shu. "Which means they are now, at this moment, three centuries more advanced than that."

"Yes," agreed Vecchio.

"So, they have probably developed beyond our own level of technology."

"Potentially correct," said Vecchio.

"This goes to my earlier point," Petry chimed in. "Our journey will take over three hundred years. So—"

"Three hundred forty-five," corrected Achebe, the pilot/navigator.

"Give or take a few months," the co-pilot, Grussmacher, added.

"Though," said Vecchio, "due to time dilation, almost seven hundred years will have passed here on Earth, and on Kyra-2B."

"*So...*" Petry repeated the word forcefully and paused to ensure he had the floor. "The aliens will be roughly a thousand years into their future when compared to where they were when we received those messages."

"That is more or less correct," said Vecchio. "In any event, you should expect a far more advanced civilization."

"How much more?"

"For an approximation, I'd suggest looking back to

our own technology ten centuries in the past."

Petry shuddered. "No running water? Separate shacks for bathrooms?"

"Outhouses," Worona said mildly. She served the dual role of team doctor and biologist. "That's what they called them."

"Disgusting is what I call them," Petry said. "My point is, if the Kyrans are going to be that much more advanced when we arrive, how dangerous will that be for us?"

"Potentially very." Vecchio spoke in a flat tone.

"That sounds like a reason to wait before galloping off to say hello," said Petry.

"Or a good reason to immediately do so," argued Grussmacher.

Kemper didn't interfere with the exchange. Variances of it had been occurring all over the world since the discovery of the Kyrans. Some counseled a cautious approach, whether because they feared the potential military might of the aliens or out of a scientific desire to learn as much as possible before acting. However, the urgency of the situation on earth drove others to support a near-immediate response. The prospect of technology exchange loomed large for the scientific-minded. The possibility of another habitable planet convinced others. A faction of the military-centric favored action and actively gaining intelligence at the source over passive observation.

"Contacting an alien species blind is certainly dangerous," conceded Vecchio. "But this entire mission is dangerous. For example, as the physicists will cover later today, simply traveling through space at point-eight-seven of light speed is also quite dangerous."

Petry's frown deepened. "I'm an engineer. I don't need a sociologist to explain space travel to me. I know the risks that come with it. Even cryo-stasis is estimated to have a thirty percent failure rate. But those are *processes*. I understand how they work. It's people I'm unsure about. Or whatever you want to call these creatures."

Vecchio gave no indication his interruption annoyed her in the least. "It's a valid consideration. However, consider this: Kyra-2B is in the top three percent of planets we've discovered that are reasonably Earth-like. Their atmosphere is richer in oxygen than ours currently, but falls well within the range of oxygen levels that have existed here in past eons. The Kyrans themselves resemble homo sapiens in several key areas. It appears they are bipedal, for example. Unlike our own current state of the hominids here on earth, of which we are the only remaining branch, we believe Kyra-2B is home to multiple species. For comparison, imagine if modern-day versions of Neanderthal, Denisovans, or even Paranthropus robustus still existed here on earth."

Kemper glanced around at the crew. Most took in the news with stoic expressions, though Shu appeared fascinated. Conversely, Petry's lip curled as he listened.

"As the Kyrans appear to have developed along similar lines as our own species, at least if considered in larger spectrum of biological evolution," continued Vecchio, "it is entirely plausible their culture likewise has many parallels."

"Not exactly reassuring," noted Petry.

Vecchio shrugged. "All of this is speculation, of course," she cautioned. "We've inferred a great deal from the waves we intercepted."

"Let us remember, inference is heavily influenced by our own biases," said Worona. It was one of the first times the soft-spoken woman had entered into a conversation. As team doctor and biology expert, she carried herself with a quiet confidence.

Petry grinned broadly at her input, clearly taking it as an affirmation of his previous points. He crossed his arms triumphantly and turned his gaze to Vecchio for her response.

The woman appeared unruffled, however. "So it is," she replied, and moved on.

3

Once all the briefings were completed, the psychologists had their go at the team.

Unlike the various tests during the screening process prior to selection, which focused on eliminating unsuitable candidates, this time the doctors keyed on psychological hardening. While there were some team-based exercises, the bulk of this stage in the process was conducted in one-on-one sessions. Therapy sessions were no exception, with the results being examined by the psychological team and Dr. Worona. As captain, he would be briefed on the progress of the other crew members, but this status didn't exempt him from undergoing the therapy sessions as well.

"How are you adapting to the impact of time passage?" Dr. Selby asked Kemper during their third meeting.

The doctor was a middle-aged woman, thin to the point of boniness. Her skeletal appearance was belied by an odd sort of detached warmth Kemper found comforting. He imagined he was already equating the feeling to how Earth itself might feel to him upon his return.

"It's still a bit of a mind spin," he admitted.

"In what way?"

"In that we—I—have always viewed time as a constant. A month at my house in Ireland is the same as a month here in Texas. Once you get on a spaceship, things get... odd."

"Relativity isn't exactly a new concept," Selby observed.

"No, but it hasn't been a reality until recently, at least in the sense I mean. The technology for near light speed travel is only what, seven years old?"

Selby nodded.

Kemper recalled all of the excitement around the scientific breakthrough. The grand ideas of exploration that were discussed immediately. The mysteries that could be resolved. The discoveries they might make.

Then, like someone standing in front of the glass at an ice cream parlor, science collectively ran headlong into the choice paradox. First, it manifested as choice paralysis. So many options that the decision to commit to one brought about massive fear of missing out on the unchosen options. This continued for close to two years, while scholars and scientists and leaders all debated. During that time, the new technology was only harnessed for local system exploration. Kemper spent the latter part of his career in this period and had begun to wonder if humans would ever deign to travel outside the solar system. Like a bull kicking at the corral gate and finally knocking it down, the species stood frozen at the opening, suddenly intimidated by the great wide world outside its pen.

After a while, the legitimate debates ended, and the squabbling began. The resources necessary to mount an extra-solar system expedition were considerable for an already heavily taxed planet. Those resources made available to the CSA as the pooling entity for those resources were deemed minimally adequate. Within the organization's walls, every scientist and member nation alike seemed to have a pet project. All of them vied to be in first position and none had enough consensus to reach it. The resulting stalemate resembled the electoral convention of a divided political party.

The discovery of life on Kyra-2B resolved this conflict, at least temporarily. Finally, an answer to the Fermi Paradox—*if life is abundant in the universe, where is everybody?*—was found. This first indication of intelligent life elsewhere in the galaxy proved galvanizing enough to unite the disputing parties when it came to the maiden expedition, even if the majority who agreed did so for radically different reasons. Regardless of whether the impetus was for discovery, defense, colonization, or to stave off existential crisis, humanity was finally united enough to select a mission.

"Even over the past seven years," Kemper said, "relativity hasn't been part of our everyday lives. I mean, sure, we all experience the sense of time dragging or flying by, depending on how much we are engrossed in an activity. But that is perception. With this expedition, we're dealing with something else entirely. Time will literally pass differently."

"What about that bothers you?"

"I don't know that it does. It's difficult for a lay person like me to get my head around, that's all. My pilots don't seem to have an issue with it at all."

"Why do you suppose that is?"

"They understand it better."

"You don't?"

Kemper thought about it. "I do. I had to put it into terms that made sense to me."

"What are those?"

"I break it down by location."

Selby raised a brow.

"It's simpler that way," Kemper said. "Look, the time our vessel will take to travel from Earth to Kyra is 345 years. That's objective travel time, okay?"

"Yes," said Selby.

"Good. For me and my crew, far fewer years will pass. We'll spend the majority of that in cryo, so we'll only experience a few months of that journey, at most."

Selby nodded. "That is one of the impacts for which I am preparing your psyche."

"I think that's the easy part," said Kemper. "We'll be focused on the mission, so none of that other stuff will really come to bear until we return."

"By other stuff, you mean the passage of time here on Earth."

"Yes."

"Six hundred ninety-seven years," Selby specified.

"Yes. Plus another six ninety-seven on the return trip. That's almost fourteen hundred years. By the time we return from our mission, the technology we used to travel to Kyra-2B will have been obsolete by centuries."

"That is entirely likely."

"It's a near certainty," Kemper corrected. "One that's difficult to imagine. It'd be like sending someone exploring out to sea in a dugout canoe, only for them to return a year later to see massive battleships and tankers in the harbor, with a modern cityscape behind them." Kemper thought for a moment. "And planes flying overhead."

"It sounds disconcerting."

"Walking in on your parents is disconcerting. This is… barely conceivable. Not only will technology have changed, but we—the crew and I—will be obsolete upon return. We'll be relics. Even our language will be essentially extinct."

"Quite possibly," Selby agreed. "How are you processing that?"

Kemper drew in a deep breath and let it out. "I think of it as a form of time travel. We aren't just going to Kyra-2B. We're going into the future."

Selby considered his words. Finally, she nodded her approval. "I think that is an entirely healthy way to approach this scenario. The largest difficulty I anticipate for you and your crew is the ability to let go of the past."

Kemper grinned. "That won't be a problem, Doctor. Aside from my house, I'm not leaving anything behind that losing it will devastate me."

"You say that," Selby told him, "but you may not be prepared for the immensity of the emotions when they occur in the moment."

"I'll be fine." He glanced at her. "Honestly, what I

want most out of our sessions is to help me prepare for how to handle my crew's reactions."

Selby was silent for a few moments. Then she said, "I can't predict with any degree of certainty how each member will react. Interstellar travel is a new experience, and the data set is nonexistent."

"You wouldn't compare it to Intra-stellar experience, then?"

Selby shook her head. "Despite extended travel time in that instance, there is little time juxtaposition, and cryo-stasis. This type of experiential stimuli tends to manifest quite differently in the travelers psychology. It isn't the same at all."

The statement made sense to Kemper. He'd logged enough time traveling within the solar system to know the doctor was correct. "What about coma patients?" he asked. "Ones that wake up after years of being unconscious?"

Selby considered briefly. "There is some parallel, I suppose. But the scale is nowhere near the same. There is simply no comparable data to the effect of the type of extended stasis you and your crew will face."

"Take a stab, then," Kemper urged. "Do your best."

"Some may be unaffected," Selby allowed, "as you expect to be yourself. Though, I would caution you to be prepared for another reaction entirely."

"Noted."

"Others," said Selby, "may experience various degrees of depression or develop a nihilistic or hedonistic mindset."

Kemper nodded. That made sense to him.

"Can I expect anything more severe?"

"The possibility of a psychotic break always exists. When the mind is unable to process events or concepts, there is a danger of this response. Time dilation has the potential to create a great deal of cognitive dissonance. We have done what we can to mitigate the possibility of a mental breakdown."

"You can't eliminate it?"

"No. Not entirely."

Kemper shrugged. In addition to the phenomenon of time dilation, they'd be dealing with first contact with an alien species. He suspected *that* would be considerably more taxing on the crew's mental state. Something else occurred to him and he smiled slightly.

"What is it?" Selby asked.

"I just realized," Kemper said, "by the time I'm putting your advice to use, you'll be long gone. Back to the dust, as it were."

Selby didn't seem bothered by his observation. "That fate awaits us all," she said evenly. "I do envy you your coming experiences, though."

"Which part? Meeting alien life for the first time, or seeing our future?"

"Both," said Selby. "You are being afforded two incredible moments in human history."

"Want to switch places, Doctor?"

Selby almost cracked a smile. "Not on your life."

The crew spent the next several months training and cross-training. The basic skills of each member were presented to the team as a whole. Everyone learned how to perform these skills in rudimentary fashion. This practice was an age-old redundancy, hearkening back to the days of military special forces. This element of their training served as a quiet reminder of two seemingly contradictory facts: each of the crew members was essential and any one of them may not survive this mission.

Meanwhile, other astronaut teams spent months handling the multiple launches of shuttles that carried the modular spacecraft pieces needed to assemble the spacecraft the crew would use to travel to Kyra-2B. As each piece reached orbit, it was added to the previous ones to eventually create the whole, which was dubbed *Doncella*, the Spanish word for *maiden*. Gupta had suggested "maiden" as an appropriate name for a vessel making the first ever voyage outside the solar system. Shu made the point that, since the crew was lacking a Hispanic member, perhaps using the language for the ship's name could remedy that omission. Kemper agreed and the vessel was christened thusly.

Petry balked at the idea of others assembling the components of the ship. In particular, he worried over the installation of the Meitner drive, which made their near-light speed possible. However, Kemper wasn't bothered. He saw this as part of the natural process of collaboration. An engineer designed the various parts, and another technician manufactured and assembled them. The astronaut transport team, a multi-national effort every bit as diverse as his own crew, was simply the last step on the assembly line. He didn't bother using this logic with Petry, however. Instead, he merely assured the engineer he would have ample time to check over the work of his peers before they accelerated from sub-light.

Kemper watched his crew during the training period. He saw how they came together as a professional unit, despite their differences. The deliberate effort each member took to ensure this result became a source of pride for Kemper. He noticed more subtle dynamics, as well. The push-pull of the collaborative relationship between the pilot/navigator Achebe and his co-pilot, the younger Grussmacher. Petry's not-so-veiled romantic overtures toward Shu and, when she rebuffed him, toward Worona, who likewise brushed them aside. Yet none of the three seemed to harbor any bitterness over the exchange. He admired the way the crew members argued passionately about the different factions and philosophies surrounding this mission without anyone becoming truly angry.

Solid, he thought. They were solid.

Thus, when Director Vasim Gupta informed him the *Doncella* was assembled and fully prepared for departure and asked him how he assessed his crew's preparation, he answered without any reservation.

"Sir, we are good to go."

"Any last-minute assignment changes?" asked the director.

Kemper shook his head. "The primary crew is ready."

"Then say goodbye to the reserve pool, and pack your bags for Florida, Captain."

Kemper snapped a salute, even though Gupta was a

civilian. "Yes, sir!"

The shuttle liftoff from Florida went off without a hitch.

In orbit, they rendezvoused with *Doncella*. There was a brief filmed ceremony for PR purposes during which time his crew exchanged places with the astronauts responsible for the final stage of assembly. From the mission control center, Director Gupta put on his public face and made some pronouncements. As the oncoming Captain, Kemper asked the ranking technician for permission to come aboard and accepted the transfer of command. His crew stood nearby, waiting stoically.

He suspected they were all as eager to get underway as he was.

Once the pomp and circumstance was completed and the assembly team had departed, the crew set about final preparations. Kemper gave Petry two full days to check and recheck all systems. Achebe and Grussmacher calculated their trajectory for the hundredth time. Since her primary expertise wouldn't be pertinent until they reached their destination, Shu assisted wherever she was needed. Worona monitored the crew while likewise pitching in.

Kemper oversaw it all.

On the third day, Petry engaged the engines, and Achebe set them on a course out of the solar system. They remained at low speed for several weeks, checking communication, structural integrity, and confirming the scores of previous checks on every other system. Redundancies ensured nothing was missed. Though not all had astronaut experience, redundancy also provided a form of comfort to their scientific selves.

As the ship passed through the path of Neptune's orbit, Kemper assembled the crew on the small observation deck. The six of them gazed through the narrow window slit at three bright lights in the distance. Venus outshined the other two, but there was no mistaking which was Earth.

Kemper had never been this far from his own planet before. To see it resembling nothing more than a bright, non-twinkling star was slightly jarring. The fact this was only the beginning of the journey injected another emotion he couldn't identify. Sadness? Excitement? Trepidation?

All three, he suspected, with a twist of bittersweet added to the mix.

The group was silent for a long while, each alone with their thoughts. He felt Shu's shoulder pressing lightly against his while he stared at Earth.

"Captain?" Worona said. "A few words, perhaps?"

Kemper nodded. He'd given some thought to what to say in this moment. Ultimately, he decided that simple was best.

He cleared his throat and spoke.

"Our home will be here for us when we return, though greatly changed. I imagine we'll be changed, as well. Either way, say a fond goodbye to the Earth you know before we turn our focus to the mission before us."

He paused, and several crew members muttered a farewell in their native tongues. Then he continued.

"For our part, let's remember an old Irish sailing

prayer." Kemper let the hint of a smile touch his lips as he spoke. "May the seas lie smooth before us. May a gentle breeze forever fill our sails. May sunshine warm our faces, and kindness warm our souls."

There was another moment of reverent silence. Once Kemper felt it had gone on long enough, he gave the next order.

"Mr. Petry, prepare the Meitner drive for maximum velocity."

"Aye, sir."

"Everyone else," Kemper said, "strap in."

Harnessing the energy to reach .87c was a technological feat for which Kemper readily admitted he didn't understand the technical complexities. He did know what came next was one of the most dangerous stages of the mission.

"Status, Mr. Petry?"

"Meitner drive is primed and prepared for acceleration, sir."

"The Ueshiba deflectors?"

"Ready, sir."

Kemper cast a quick glance around the small bridge to ensure all members were secure at their respective stations. Then he said, "Engage the Ueshiba deflector system."

Petry eased a lever forward almost lovingly. "Engaged, sir."

"System check?"

"Functioning at full capacity."

Kemper turned to Grussmacher. "Confirm course, Navigator."

"Confirmed." Grussmacher's even tone carried a hint of excitement.

"Very well. Mr. Petry, you may increase power to the Meitner drive at ten percent intervals."

"Aye, sir."

Petry punched several buttons on the screen and then slowly eased his finger upward. Kemper felt the thrum of energy course throughout the ship as he did so.

"Point-eight-seven light speed is now capable, sir," Petry pronounced. "Sub-light engines are offline."

Kemper turned his gaze to Achebe. "You may accelerate, Pilot. Same intervals – ten percent."

Achebe nodded solemnly. He manipulated the screen in front of him. The ship rumbled and shook momentarily, then became still. Points of light on the viewscreen slowly extended into smudged streaks.

"Accelerating," Achebe said, though the fact was obvious.

"Deflection?" Kemper asked.

"One hundred percent efficiency," Grussmacher reported immediately.

Kemper let himself relax slightly. The true test was when they reached full acceleration but, if the Ueshiba deflection system was holding steady now, that bode well for the remainder of the journey.

Over the next two hours, Achebe reported the speed intervals as the *Doncella* eclipsed each one—point one, point two, and continuing until they passed point eight. Eventually, the pilot spoke with a satisfied air when he announced, "Point Eight Six Eight, sir."

Kemper glanced at Grussmacher, who flashed a thumbs up.

Kemper nodded. "Excellent. Way to get this mission off on the right foot."

Once the *Doncella* was at maximum velocity, another round of systems checks was performed.

Kemper knew this was largely unnecessary. If the ship was going to burst apart, the most likely moment was as soon as they accelerated. Since that didn't occur, the structural integrity proved itself sufficient to weather the rigors of travel at this speed. As long as they didn't crash into large, unmapped debris, they should arrive at Kyra-2B intact. Given the vast emptiness that was space, Kemper knew their odds were favorable.

After the systems checks were complete, the crew sat down for a final meal prior to cryogenic insertion.

He hadn't known what to expect during this meal. Would the crew be quiet and contemplative or festive? In the end, the result leaned toward the former, though there was a fair amount of banal chatter. Kemper took that as another good sign. They were nervous but confident, as he read it.

The meal complete, they began cryogenic insertion. The order of insertion, and eventually reanimation, was precisely chosen based on crew roles at the particular stage of the mission.

Ouyang Shu had the smallest role at the moment, so she went in first. Prior to stepping into the bedchamber,

Shu took each crew member's hand one by one and gave it a gentle squeeze. Then she climbed into the bed lay back. The cryo chamber was sealed and the suspended animation process initiated. Within minutes, Shu was still, her vital signs diminished but constant.

"Sleep well," Kemper said, more for the remaining crew than for Shu, who he doubted could hear him.

One by one, the others took their turn. Grussmacher went next, his redundancy as co-pilot driving his placement. Petry followed, despite his grumblings that the engineer was the most important member of the crew if something went wrong. Achebe went after him, leaving Kemper alone with Worona, the doctor and biologist. Her role here was pivotal, to oversee the process and ensure the crew's health throughout.

It made Kemper nervous that he wouldn't be the final insertion, though the logic was unassailable. He fidgeted with the temperature controlling bodysuit he wore prior to entering the chamber.

Worona seemed to sense his mood. He knew she had secondary degrees in psychology, which made her an ideal candidate for the role as team doctor. "Systems are functioning perfectly," she said.

"I know."

"You'll be the first to wake up," she assured him.

Kemper stared at the chamber, not answering. He felt an overwhelming sense of loneliness. A moment later, Worona's hand settled on his shoulder, and she squeezed. He turned to her.

"It'll be all right, Captain," the doctor said

confidently.

Kemper nodded. She was right. He took a final deep breath, then settled into the chamber. As he lay back, the compartment first closed and then sealed. He met Worona's dark eyes. The woman smiled at him reassuringly through the glass. Then there was a hiss of air, and Kemper plunged into darkness.

4

Tears streamed down Kemper's face.

Baw, baw.

A query flashed on the inside of his chamber.

COMPLETE REANIMATION?

Kemper selected YES.

At first, there seemed to be no response from the system, other than the alarm's sudden cessation. Then the query disappeared and was replaced by a notation that reanimation was in process, so Kemper waited. He filled and emptied his lungs and wriggled his fingers and toes some more.

A slight pop was followed by a light hiss and a comparative rush of air. Slowly the frosted glass rose and turned, leaving him an open path to exiting the bedchamber. Kemper flexed his leg, half-expecting it to remain frozen in place, but the muscles obeyed his command. He crawled awkwardly out of the cryo-pod, standing tentatively on the deck of the ship. His entire body felt weak and unsteady, so he reached out and held onto the edge of the cryo chamber. He took a few more deep breaths and glanced around.

The crew, he thought. That was the next step.

He half-shuffled, half-staggered to the monitoring console. Even over the short trip of several meters, he could sense his muscles adapting and strengthening. It wouldn't be long before he was fully recovered.

With some trepidation, he looked at the monitor. Losing a crew member during cryo was something Vasim Gupta and the psychologist Selby had prepared him for. There was simply no way of knowing how well the system would hold up to space travel and the passage of time. Petry's estimate of potential cryo failure running as high as thirty percent wasn't hyperbole. Losing a crew member at this stage was a very real risk.

His eyes swept over the screen.

All systems green.

Kemper let out a breath he hadn't realized he was holding in. His finger snaked out to Worona's controls and he initiated her reanimation process.

While the system slowly brought the doctor out of cryo, Kemper used the time to check the navigator's station. His understanding of the equipment didn't approach that of Achebe or Grussmacher, but he could read it well enough to gauge their location. The *Doncella* was on course for—and nearing the solar system of—Kyra-2B.

His reanimation had been triggered exactly as planned.

Worona seemed to recover from cryo even more quickly than he had. Kemper recalled that the less mass a person had, the swifter the process. Something to do with the amount of muscle tissue and volume of blood. The difference wasn't extreme, but noticeable.

After a series of deep knee bends and some gentle hopping, Worona turned to Kemper and smiled. "Shall we wake the rest?"

Each crew member responded slightly differently to reanimation. Where Worona had been spry and almost jocular, both Achebe and Grussmacher were more reserved. Petry was outright morose and sluggish. Only Shu seemed virtually unaffected.

Once everyone was present, Kemper ordered a cursory systems check. When all emergency systems came back as functioning with normal parameters the crew took the opportunity to change into uniforms. As he dressed, Kemper decided a quick meal should be the next order of business. A counterpoint to the last supper they'd shared before cryo, he figured. The crew accepted the decision without argument, though Petry frowned at the delay. The engineer clearly wanted to dive deeper into the diagnostics of the ship and especially the Meitner drive.

While they ate, Kemper probed for psychological impact. He avoided referring to home or to the fact that six and a half centuries had passed there in the time they'd been asleep. There'd been enough Rip Van Winkle jokes during training he didn't make any attempts at humor, either. Instead, he focused on the mission ahead, and evaluated the state of mind of each member of the crew.

"We'll check the deceleration calculations right after breakfast," Achebe assured him. The man remained as stoic as he'd been throughout training, and his steadiness seemed to buoy others. "Grussmacher will run them and I will re-run them. We need a couple of hours and we'll be ready."

Kemper sipped some orange juice, nodding his approval. When his gaze shifted to Petry, the engineer's frown didn't falter. "I'm ready now," he assured Kemper. "We can decelerate whenever you order, Captain."

He turned to Worona.

The doctor was chewing a dense biscuit. She finished and swallowed before answering. "I'd like to conduct a physical for each crew member but that can wait until we've completed deceleration. Based on visual examination, I'm not seeing any immediate concerns."

"Thank you, Doctor." Kemper looked at Shu. He didn't expect the cosmic anthropologist to have anything to report, but still gave her the opportunity as a matter of group dynamics. Every crew member should be included.

Shu flashed him a smile. "I'm excited to meet the Kyrans soon," was all she said.

"Me, too," said Kemper. Then he raised his juice in the air. The others followed suit, and he offered a toast. "Here's to all of us still being here," he said. "A trend I intend to make sure continues. Cheers!"

"*Gan Bei!*" Shu responded, lifting her glass slightly higher.

Grussmacher jabbed his box in the air. "*Prost!*"

Petry gave a reluctant "*Na zdravie,*" and lowered his drink.

"*Impilo,*" intoned Achebe in his deep voice.

"*L'Chaim*," said Worona quietly.

Everyone drank.

"Confirm deceleration calculations, Navigator," Kemper said.

"Confirmed," said Grussmacher.

"Seconded," Achebe added immediately.

"You may decelerate, Pilot," Kemper said.

Achebe worked the lever, slowly returning it to the lowered position over the next two hours. With Grussmacher's assistance, he adjusted the timing of the deceleration increments at each interval. Eventually, the *Doncella* shuddered for a few milliseconds, then stabilized. Stars that had been short, streaky smudges a moment before snapped into sharp, pinpoint focus.

"Engaging sub-light engines," Grussmacher stated, without waiting for the order. A moment later, he confirmed, "Engaged."

"Our location, Navigator?"

Achebe read the screen before replying. "We are currently 27.6 AU from Kyra-2B, sir."

Kemper raised an appreciative brow. Their target had been twenty-nine, roughly the same distance as from Earth to Neptune. In cosmic terms, Achebe and Grussmacher had barely missed the mark.

"Communications?"

Grussmacher slid to the communication station. "Several messages from home, sir."

Kemper experienced a moment of dissonance. Although he knew that the messages had traveled at light speed while the Doncella had only reached .87 of that velocity, it was still mildly jarring to have messages queued and waiting.

"Any of them priority one?" he asked Grussmacher, shaking off the sensation of strangeness.

"No, sir," the pilot responded. "All are priority three."

Priority three designated the messages as personal or routine. "Save those for later," Kemper said. "Anything from Kyra-2B?"

Grussmacher scanned the screen, his expression perplexed. "The system has mostly logged similar traffic to what was originally received on Earth prior to our departure. Intended for their own civilization, in other words. However, the AI has flagged one message that was sent..." He paused, and frowned.

"What is it?" Kemper asked.

"I'm just trying to figure out which time context to use, sir."

"Ground it to Kyra-2B," Kemper ordered. "Consider their initial transmission date as year zero."

Grussmacher hit a few keys. "Done. Using that time benchmark, the flagged message was broadcast one hundred sixteen years after the initial signals we first received on Earth."

"How did the system flag it?"

"The other signals are labeled as within civilization," said Grussmacher. "AI analysis has determined this was a message intended for... well, extraterrestrial life, sir."

"For us, you mean." Kemper rubbed his chin. This was interesting. "Put the message on the main display."

Grussmacher complied. A moment later, a simple diagram filled the main viewer. Several crew members gasped involuntarily.

"Oh, my," Shu said quietly, her tone full of wonder.

The image of three separate bi-pedal species were represented on the screen. All had legs with knees that bent the opposite direction as humans, along with several noticeable joints below the knee. The hands featured opposable thumbs but only three fingers. Significant differences existed between each of the species, especially in terms of size and build. The tallest and most lithe of the three also had the largest heads, including dark eyes, no discernible nose or ears. A second species was nearly half as tall and stouter, with a smaller head. The third looked to be midway between the other two in terms of height but was considerably thicker and more muscularly defined. The thumb appeared more like a claw on the hands of this third species.

The first, taller species held its hand up at an angle across its chest. The arms of the other two dangled at their sides. Gill-like flaps existed on the sides of the heads of all three species, though Kemper couldn't determine their purpose. Was this civilization primarily aquatic?

He turned to Shu. He was tempted to ask for her analysis but resisted the urge. He gave both her and Worona an opportunity to examine the images and turned back to take in the rest.

Symbols he assumed represented language filled a portion of the screen. Kemper also recognized common geometric designs, including pi. He nodded slowly in appreciation. Astronomers had long opined math might be the universal language, at least among those planets with similar biomes to earth.

He glanced at Petry, who was staring at the designs with the same expression of wonder as both Shu and Worona.

"It's their equivalent of a Voyager greeting," Shu said, almost reverently.

Kemper sat quietly for a long while, letting the crew soak in this message. The significance of it wasn't lost upon him. That the Kyrans had sent a purposeful broadcast intended for extraterrestrial intelligence meant they had reached a level of technological maturity akin to their own.

It was an exceedingly good sign.

"Shu?" Kemper finally asked quietly. "Do you think you can translate the glyphs?"

"Given time," she answered confidently.

"What do you make of the three species?"

"Early interpretations of the messages we intercepted on Earth hinted at this," Shu said. "Based on this message, it appears the taller species are most likely the ones who created this."

"Why do you say that?"

"They are in a position of primacy, for one. Also, that figure is the only one posed in a gesture of salutation." Shu spoke excitedly now, staring at the screen while she answered. "But I'll have additional insight for you after I've had an opportunity to fully examine this."

"Are they warlike?" Kemper pressed.

Shu hesitated, then shook her head. "It's not overtly apparent." She glanced at him. "You know our own history, Captain, and the image we first projected to the cosmos. An alien species intercepting our Voyager message could be forgiven if they didn't suspect the level of violence the human race employed throughout our existence."

"We overcame," Kemper replied.

"Barely," muttered Petry, and Kemper saw Achebe nod in agreement.

"True," allowed Shu. "There was a dangerous period that could have gone another way. Self-destruction is, after all, considered one of the potential means that the Great Filter can manifest."

"The Great Filter," muttered Kemper.

He understood the theory well, as it had long been one of the two most accepted answers to the Fermi Paradox. The thinking went that the reason the galaxy wasn't teeming with intelligent, advanced civilizations was that there existed some event along the development path that few, if any, civilizations managed to successfully overcome. Shu's assertion that destruction by their own technology was perhaps the most popular candidate, though the volatility of a planet's geology or the vagaries of a universe that seemed to hurl chunks of rock all about the cosmos were also probabilities.

"You may be right," Kemper mused. "Based on the number of worlds we've detected capable of sustaining life, *that* availability certainly wasn't the barrier."

"That's why I've always favored abiogenesis as the culprit," Worona interjected. "It seems like the most vulnerable point in the process. Really, what's more vulnerable than that moment when the spark of life occurs?"

"Regardless," Shu said, "the point, sir, is we painted ourselves in the best possible light in our intended first message to alien life. We didn't intentionally broadcast our violent tendencies out to them."

"Those tendencies would have been apparent in our internal chatter, though," Kemper said. He turned to Grussmacher, who was staring at the images on the main screen. "Run a computer scan on the Kyrans' internal transmissions for thematic content," Kemper ordered him.

"Yes, sir." Grussmacher worked at his console for several minutes, finally shaking his head. "The AI can't detect a consistent theme," he told Kemper. "We'll need to examine individual transmissions to get a better handle on their nature."

Kemper imagined all of the varied signals that bounced around Earth—or had, at least —when they left. Those that escaped into the universe would paint a confusing portrait of the planet to outsiders. Would an alien race be able to discern entertainment fiction from the reality of human communication? Would they be able to do so with Kyran transmissions?

"Start with the most recent," Kemper told Grussmacher. "Shu, work with him. See if you can get a handle on where they are today."

Kemper turned to Petry to speak, but Grussmacher interrupted him before he could say a word.

"Sir? The most recent transmissions are plus two hundred twenty-three years."

Kemper's brow knitted. He motioned toward the

screen with the Kyran greeting displayed. "Two hundred twenty-three years after this message?"

"No, sir. After what you designated as year zero."

"So..." Kemper did a quick calculation in his head. "One hundred five years after they sent this intentional greeting."

Grussmacher nodded.

"How long ago was that?"

"Roughly seven hundred seventy years ago, Kyran time," Grussmacher said.

Kemper cocked his head. "You're telling me there've been *no* transmissions in the past nearly eight hundred years?"

Grussmacher shook his head. "Not that the system intercepted, anyway. It was set to monitor all known frequencies in use by the Kyrans when we departed Earth, as well as those our scientists suspected might be universal." Grussmacher paused a beat, before adding, "Like the hydrogen band, for instance."

Kemper leaned back, thinking. He stared up at the screen while he considered the possibilities. "So, eight hundred years ago, something happened to the Kyrans that made it impossible for them to transmit, or..."

"Or they reached a point in their civilization in which they embraced the Dark Forest philosophy," finished Shu.

Kemper knew that theory as well. It competed with the idea of the Great Filter as one of the most prominent solutions to the Fermi Paradox. The theory held that intelligent, technologically advanced civilizations *did* exist within the galaxy. However, they chose to mask their existence to avoid potential discovery from a more powerful, potentially predatory civilization.

"The Dark Forest approach is an inevitability," Petry said. "Once a species gets over the shiny new toy phase of space travel, it is the only way of thinking that makes any sense."

"The *only* way?" Worona chimed in. "How can you be that absolute?"

Petry shrugged. "Look at our own history. What has happened every time a technologically superior culture has come into contact with a less advanced one? Up until a couple hundred years ago, the story was always the same—tragedy. If we're the less advanced culture in this scenario, I think avoiding the notice of an apex civilization is the only rational response."

"That's a very human-centric interpretation," Shu said evenly. "We have no way of knowing other species will act in a similar fashion."

"The laws of physics seem to be the same everywhere in the galaxy," Petry argued. "I find it likely the motivations of intelligent life will be similar, as well."

"Even so, how does a culture go from sending out a greeting like this," Kemper pointed to the image of the Kyran greeting them on the screen, "to deciding to hide from the rest of the universe to avoid the other so-called hunters in the interstellar dark forest?"

"Cultural philosophies evolve over time," Shu told him. "It's entirely possible they received some sort of reply to their message they found... disconcerting."

"Something that made them go dark?" he asked.

Shu turned over her hands. "It's entirely plausible."

Kemper tapped the arm of his chair while he thought. "Navigator, how long until we reach Kyra-2B?"

Achebe's reply was immediate. "At present speed, twenty-six days."

"Then that's how long we have to solve this riddle," Kemper stated. "Let's get to work."

5

The days passed quickly.

While Shu worked tirelessly on the glyphs, Achebe and Grussmacher scanned Kyra-2B whenever the other was on pilot duty. Petry took the opportunity to run diagnostics on the *Doncella* on a loop. The engineer's care for the ship was borderline compulsive, but that was a trait Kemper counted as an asset in the moment.

The messages from Earth were, in terms of Earth time, nearly seven hundred years old. They contained an initial slew of well-wishes from dignitaries and leading scientists and a few personal messages. Kemper assumed these were farewells from family, based on the reactions of the various crew members. He watched for the psychological slippage Doctor Selby had drilled him on, but saw no signs of anything more than natural sadness.

Kemper received no personal messages.

There were also no messages dating more than ten years post-launch. This initially troubled Kemper, though Gupta had warned him this might be the case. Rather than fill the airwaves with one-way chatter, the director suggested that Earth may simply wait quietly for their arrival in the Kyran system.

Therefore, while the crew members attended to their duties, Kemper prepared a message.

> DONCELLA HAS ARRIVED IN THE KYRAN SYSTEM. ALL CREW MEMBERS SURVIVED JOURNEY. RECEIVED A NON-DIRECTED, GENERIC GREETING MESSAGE FROM KYRAN SPECIES. C.A. SHU ANALYZING. NO DIRECT CONTACT FROM -2B. APPROACHING PLANET AT SUB-LIGHT. REPORTS TO FOLLOW.

He initially marked it to be sent to Director Gupta, before realizing Gupta had been deceased for centuries. He modified it to simply be to the attention of Central Space Command. Then it occurred to him such an entity may no longer exist. Seven hundred years was a long time. Many countries failed to last centuries, much less mere organizations.

As his finger hovered over the send button, another thought struck him. His report would take another three hundred years to arrive on Earth. Whoever received it would be getting news of their arrival in the Kyran system a full millennia after the departure of the *Doncella.*

The weight of the situation settled on him for a moment. He considered revising his terse message with an eye toward what its impact might be on the recipient. He imagined someone in the early industrial age getting a message from Rome at the height of its power.

Would it be any more than a curiosity to them? Did they have technology now that dwarfed that which brought this crew here? Or had mankind been waiting all this time, waiting and wondering what happened to the mission of the *Doncella?*

Kemper's finger twitched. He had no answers.

A futile, lonely report, he decided, but transmitted it all the same.

That was the mission.

As the *Doncella* entered the inner solar system, slipping past a pair of binary gas giants roughly the size of Uranus, Shu still had no answers.

"I remain convinced the Elves are the origin of this message," she told Kemper, a week into her studies.

"Elves?"

"Sorry. It's a shorthand I've taken to using in my own mind." She pointed to the tall, slender Kyrans with the largest heads. "I call these the Elves. The shorter ones are the Dwarves. And these thicker bodied ones are the Orcs."

Kemper didn't know whether to be amused at the ancient Tolkien references or concerned at her third choice. "Orcs were not pleasant creatures, as I recall."

"Actually, none of them were, if you read classic Tolkien closely enough," Shu said. "Anyway, I wasn't making any sort of character judgment, just selecting a shorthand based on body type."

Kemper cracked a small grin. "It's kind of funny, if you think about it." When Shu looked at him askance, he added, "We flew three hundred light years in a spaceship to meet a bunch of fantasy creatures."

"Oh." Shu actually giggled. "Ironic, isn't it?" She pointed to one she'd labeled as the elf. "I believe they were the dominant race at the time of this message. As I mentioned before, their position of primacy is the first indicator."

"What if their culture doesn't go from top to bottom?" Kemper asked. "It's not universal, any more than reading left to right. Go pick up one of Worona's books written in Hebrew if you doubt me."

"No, of course, you're quite correct," Shu said, unperturbed. "But the few math equations we've been able to understand begin with the simplest at the top and become progressively more complex as you go downward. I think that is a good indicator of how they orient information."

"If the more complex is near the bottom," Kemper argued, "wouldn't that mean your orcs are the more evolved?"

"It's a possibility," she admitted. "There is no way to know without more data. Direct observation would obviously be the best source. But does this..." She pointed to the thin Kyran. "...really look less evolved to you..." Her finger drifted downward to the stockier, claw-thumbed orc. "...than this?"

Kemper eyed the figures for the hundredth time, trying to see them with fresh eyes. "No," he finally said.

"Not to me, either."

"Still no luck with the glyphs?" he asked, already knowing the answer but wanting to hear about some kind of progress.

"No. Linguistics is an entire discipline of its own. As an anthropologist, it is one of my tertiary skills, at best. To make matters more difficult, my skillset is based more on spoken language than written. But I believe any message sent out into the stars would contain its own key to unlocking the language. Most likely, that key is buried in the math."

"Also a tertiary skill of yours?"

"Quaternary, more like."

"If you know that word, maybe your math is better than you think."

"I wish that was the case. I've enlisted the aid of our engineer to solve the code."

"How has he done?'

"Well, when I can get him to tear himself away from the fourteenth diagnostic of the ship's systems *and* when I can convince him there likely *is* a code within the math that will serve as a Rosetta stone, he is actually quite industrious."

"But no breakthrough," Kemper said.

"Not yet."

"Keep at it," he told her, and Shu nodded in reply.

Despite the best efforts of Shu and assistance from the different crew members, she was no closer to translating the greeting or interpreting any of the ancient signals when the *Doncella* approached Kyra-2B.

Once the planet was in full view, Kemper ordered Grussmacher to establish an asynchronous orbit so the planet surface would scroll past the ship slowly enough to allow for a detailed search. "Continue your scans," he directed Achebe, who was taking a shift in the co-pilot's chair.

"Aye, sir."

Kemper stared down at the planet. It was jarring to see a blue marble before them in the dark of space, bearing an uncanny resemblance to Earth. Only the radically unfamiliar land masses below broke the comparison. A lump rose in his throat while he gazed at the planet.

"Oxygen levels are within two percent of our initial estimates prior to the expedition," Achebe reported.

"Biology readings?"

"Difficult to ascertain. Thermal signatures seem to indicate scattered life forms."

"Still no transmissions?"

"None, sir."

Kemper rubbed his chin. "Could they have found a way to mask them?"

Achebe shrugged, glancing at Petry to take on the question.

"The laws of physics are called *laws* for a reason," the engineer said. "With that said, I suppose it is possible they may have developed a way to create a dampening field of some kind. I'd still expect it to create some kind of a power signature, whether of its own accord or showing up in its impact on other objects and systems."

"Could they have found a way to more precisely deliver each wave?" Kemper asked.

Petry considered. "I suppose so. But that would be

considerably advanced technology. Beyond ours."

"They've had a thousand years to advance their science since we first received their transmissions on Earth," Shu reminded him. "A lot can happen in a thousand years. We went from Kepler and Copernicus to having the Meitner drive."

Petry frowned. "I said it was possible. I just don't think it's probable."

"Let's get across the terminator," Kemper said. "See what things look like at night."

The night was dark.

The startlingly obvious observation disappointed Kemper. He had hoped to see lights from a civilized region of the planet below. Even if the Kyrans were masking their location from other, potentially dangerous civilizations within the galaxy, he expected to see at least some small measure of evidence of their existence once night fell.

He went back to an earlier question, recalling the gill-like features on the sides of the heads of all three species. "Are they potentially aquatic?" he asked Shu. "Should we be searching the oceans?"

Shu glanced at Worona, who shrugged. "Difficult to say, sir. We see gills when we look at that organ because of our own earthly context. The function could just as easily be to detect sounds or smells or some other sense that serves an important purpose on this planet."

Shu pointed through the viewscreen. "That planet looks an awful lot like ours. What percentage of the surface is ocean?"

"Roughly sixty percent," Achebe answered.

"So, comparable to Earth. Not only that, but a bipedal form of intelligent life that is vaguely humanoid developed here. Couldn't those gills be gills, as well?"

"They could," Worona allowed, "and just as easily could not."

Kemper resisted the urge to frown. At times, scientists could be an infuriating lot.

The crew sat in silence, watching the deep black of the planet surface move slowly past. Achebe continued his scan without a word. Finally, Kemper ordered everyone to begin a sleep cycle in rotation.

"Once everyone is rested," he said, "we'll go at this again."

He dreamt of home.

Images of cities he remembered morphed into advanced skylines he imagined awaited them upon their return. His dream-self ignored this magnificence, struggling only to return to his small, stone house on the Emerald Isle. Obstacle after obstacle was flung in his path, from bureaucracy to fame to outright physical opposition. He overcame each, though the details of his solutions were murky to his dream-self. All he knew was he eventually stood in front of his home, fourteen centuries removed from when he'd seen it last.

It was nothing but rubble.

Distressed, Kemper picked among the stones strewn in the empty field where his house had stood. He searched the ground, desperate to find the coin he'd hidden in the mantle. No sign of it—or the mantle itself, for that matter—was to be found.

A dark emotion rose in Kemper's chest, some toxic mixture of rage and terrible sadness that created some new feeling, for which he had no name. He had known Earth would move forward without him. His house was supposed to remain his house.

When he woke, he did not feel rested.

Nonetheless, he slid out of his small cabin and made the short trip to the bridge. Grussmacher was at the co-pilot station, scanning. Petry was at his position, no doubt running diagnostics. Kemper bid them good morning and took his seat. Below them, the planet was still dark, but he could see the terminal line on the horizon now.

Kemper brooded on his dream long enough to expunge the emotional hangover, then turned his attention to the problem at hand. He mulled over different courses of actions, weighing the risks of each against the probable outcomes.

Once the remainder of the crew was assembled, he said, "The way I see it, we have three options. Option one is to turn the ship around now and begin the journey homeward. Option two is to remain in orbit until we believe we've gathered as much data as we're going to get, then head home. Option three is we take the *Doncellita* shuttle planet side and investigate further."

The crew was quiet, mulling over his words. Kemper gave them a minute or so, then asked Achebe, "The atmosphere is breathable?"

"Yes, sir."

"Microbe or bacterial concerns?"

"We'd need to scan for those while within the atmosphere itself," said Achebe.

Kemper turned to Petry, "Will the structural integrity of the *Doncellita* handle entry into the atmosphere?"

The engineer nodded without hesitation.

"And it carries sufficient fuel and power to achieve breakaway velocity when it's time to leave?" Kemper asked him.

Again, Petry nodded. "With a comfortable cushion," he added. "Though there's always a risk."

"All right." Kemper glanced around at the crew. "That means all three options are viable. Thoughts?"

Shu spoke first. "I strongly recommend option three," she said, with certainty. "Our mission is to make contact. We came all this way, and now we're right here."

Worona shook her head. "Option two is the best compromise between our mission directives and crew safety," the doctor said.

"We're not going to get our answers from orbit," argued Shu. She looked to Achebe and Grussmacher for support. "They've been scanning for weeks now."

"On approach," said Worona. "Not from this close."

"You're both right," Achebe said. "Between our long-range scans prior to orbit and more detailed ones since, we've already collected all of the atmospheric and surface data of significance. Unless we're going to spend a year here to examine larger trends, we've nearly reached the end of our meaningful scans."

"A terrestrial landing was always part of the mission parameters," Shu said.

"If possible," Worona clarified, "and safe."

"Petry has confirmed it is," said Shu. "Since there currently appears to be no communication from the Kyrans to offer or deny permission, it is up to the captain's discretion."

"Something significant has changed since our mission parameters were established," said Worona. The doctor's expression seemed unduly grim. "Either the civilization has withdrawn or it has collapsed."

"Or gone extinct," Petry chimed in.

"If they've disappeared, that is another matter entirely," said Worona. "However, if the Kyrans have merely withdrawn and we force contact, wouldn't that action be considered aggressive?" She turned to Shu for confirmation.

The cosmic anthropologist nodded reluctantly. "The potential exists. We will need to be very clear in our intentions."

Worona pointed toward her and nodded before continuing. "If their civilization has collapsed, then the situation becomes even more dangerous. We could be dropping down into the middle of a second stone age or something."

"There may have been a mass exodus," Achebe suggested quietly.

Worona didn't miss a beat. "That is functionally the same as having died out. In either case, our first contact mission is scrubbed, and our only remaining directive is to determine viability for colonization, which we can do from orbit." She turned her attention to Kemper. "Sir, any of these possibilities represents too much of a risk to the crew. Remember, our goal has always been to return home after making contact."

"Home?" Grussmacher interjected. "When we get back, almost fourteen centuries will have passed. It won't be home anymore."

"Earth will always be home," said Worona.

"You might feel that way, but they won't. We talked about this in briefings before launch. We'll be like a bunch of Neanderthals, returning while paddling our way in a dugout log canoe." He glanced at Shu for support, clearly expecting her to return the favor.

Shu was hesitant. "A better analogy might be the Romans or Sui dynasty. Although, given the exponential rate of technological progress..."

Grussmacher waved away the distinction. "The point is, they'll see us as primitives. We shouldn't come back with nothing." He stared pointedly at Kemper. "Captain, I didn't come three hundred light years to leave empty-handed."

"That's a rather cowboy outlook for a scientist," chided Worona.

"I'm not a scientist. I'm a pilot."

"Achebe?" Kemper asked, forestalling Worona's reply and short-circuiting further argument. He didn't need to hear more. He understood where the two stood. Now, he wanted to know what the rest of the crew thought.

Achebe swiveled slowly in his seat to face Kemper. When he spoke, the rich baritone of his voice filled the room. "I am also a pilot. As such, my primary focus is getting this ship and crew safely to its destination and returning it home. Taking the shuttle planet side represents any number of potential dangers, ranging from mechanical failure to intervention from the Kyrans if they are in hiding, for whatever reason. Thus, my recommendation is option one."

"Not option two?"

"There is little distinction, sir. I believe the majority of the scans outlined in option two have been fulfilled. We can certainly scan fully before our departure to confirm the viability of this planet to sustain human life. But my recommendation is we do not go planet side."

Kemper nodded his understanding. He turned to Petry, giving him a questioning look.

The engineer appeared uncomfortable. "Whatever these aliens used to think," he grumbled, "they aren't looking for contact any longer. Or they aren't there at all. Either way, there's no need to risk entry and exit into the atmosphere when there seems to be nothing down there worth seeing."

To his left, Kemper heard Shu's disapproving exhale.

Petry didn't seem to notice. He stared back at Kemper. "To be absolutely clear, I concur with Achebe, Captain."

Kemper leaned back in his chair, considering. Three votes to return now, two to explore further. In the end, only his decision mattered, though. That was chain of command. He had the authority to decide and the responsibility for the outcome. He gazed down at the planet surface, watching the line of light at the terminator grow slowly closer. His choice became clear to him.

We are explorers. We've come three hundred light years. And there are still too many questions.

"Sir?" Shu said. "If I may—"

Kemper held up his hand, cutting her off. "I've heard all of you. Here's what we're going to do. Achebe will remain aboard the *Doncella* while the rest of us take the *Doncellita* and make entry into the atmosphere. If there are any land-based urban structures, we are going to find them and investigate further. Meanwhile, I want scans of the oceans in case what looks like gills on these beings actually *are* gills." He met Achebe's gaze. "You remain in orbit. We'll maintain contact at set intervals. Your standing orders are to wait for our return. However, if the situation changes, I am counting on your discretion. If we are unable to return for any reason, you have to make the return trip alone. Understood?"

Achebe nodded grimly.

"As for the rest of us," Kemper said, "is the mission clear?"

Almost as one, the crew responded, "Aye."

6

Entry was rough.

In order to employ atmospheric braking, the *Doncellita* wasn't equipped with Ueshiba deflectors like its parent craft. Therefore, the process resulted in a bumpy flight filled with friction and heat. It struck Kemper as counterintuitive that landing on a planet would be a more chaotic process than flying through almost a hundred parsecs of interstellar space. He had little time to dwell on the thought as Grussmacher managed their descent and, once in the lower atmosphere, leveled off their flight path.

"Status check," Kemper said automatically, though he knew Petry was already at work.

"Structural integrity is intact," the engineer reported a few moments later.

"Do you foresee any issues achieving escape velocity when it comes time to return to the *Doncella*?"

Petry's answer took several moments while his fingers danced over the control board. "Structural integrity is good, as I said. Engines functioning within operating parameters. As long as our fuel levels remain above sixty-two percent, I see no issues."

"Sixty-two percent?" Worona asked.

"Leaving a planet takes a lot more energy than landing on one," Petry said tersely.

"Current fuel level?" Kemper asked.

"Ninety-four percent."

Kemper turned to Grussmacher. "Let's find a city, then."

They dropped to an altitude of fifteen hundred meters and began scanning. While Shu utilized the *Doncellita's* systems, Kemper and the rest did things the old fashioned way—a visual scan.

An hour passed. Outside the craft, Kemper saw nothing but savannah wilderness. No structures, no roads. He directed Grussmacher to increase speed so they could cover more ground.

Several hours later, Shu suggested a heading for a destination about forty minutes away. "Thermal readings are higher and clustered," she explained. "Could be decaying fauna, of course, or just a herd of grazing animals, but..."

"It's better than the wasteland we're looking at now," Kemper agreed. "Let's check it out."

Shu's target was both a miss and a hit.

The clumped thermal readings turned out to be a herd of apparent herbivores, milling around the plain, their heads lowered to the grass. When the shuttle drew near, heads popped up to attention, keying on the approaching vessel. After several moments of stillness, the beasts reacted almost as one. The herd broke and ran to the east.

"Not the population center you were hoping for?" Petry remarked, his tone lightly sarcastic.

"Do you want to me to follow them, sir?" Grussmacher asked.

Kemper considered. "No. Wild animals are unlikely to flee toward civilized areas."

"It's possible they might be domesticated," Shu suggested. "Like the cattle of yesteryear on Earth. They were allowed to roam free over a vast range."

"True," Kemper agreed. "However large those pastures were, they were still fenced in. I haven't seen anything resembling a fence line. Have you?"

"No," Shu admitted.

"Continue west," Kemper ordered.

Grussmacher held his course. Within twenty minutes, off to the northwest, the broken ruins of a city, too far gone to be detected from their orbital scans, slowly became visible in the distance.

Kemper felt a mild surge of adrenaline at the sight. Grussmacher didn't need to be told to reduce speed or to head toward the city. He glanced toward Kemper as they drew near the outskirts of the ruins.

"Do a fly-over," Kemper instructed. "Watch for defensive weaponry."

Grussmacher kept the craft on course and flew directly over the remains of the alien city.

Kemper peered downward along with his crew. From this vantage point, he couldn't determine what had caused the damage to the broken structures. Was it war? Natural disaster? The ravages of time? Or some combination of all three?

"Thermal readings?" he asked Shu.

"Present, but scattered," she replied.

"Oxygen?"

"Same reading as from orbit, sir. Slightly richer than Earth."

"Radiation?"

She paused, reading the screen. "Within safe parameters."

Kemper considered for a few moments. Then he spotted a large open space within the city center. He pointed it out to Grussmacher. "Room to land?"

The pilot grinned. "I can land her on a turtle's back, sir."

"Set us down, then. Doctor Worona, scan further for allergens, carcinogens, or any harmful micro-organisms."

"Aye, sir."

Grussmacher looped around and engaged the retro thrusters. With ease, he lowered the craft to the surface, the landing apparatus thumping lightly on the ground. He powered down the engines and switched to auxiliary power systems.

Kemper unstrapped from his seat. He glanced around at the team, making a decision about mission assignment almost immediately.

"Petry will remain with the *Doncellita*," he said.

The engineer nodded his understanding. Kemper chose him as a form of safety net for the entirety of the crew. He was their most important asset when it came to returning to orbit. Not only could the engineer manage any shuttle repairs should they become necessary, but he could fly the craft if needed. Technically, so could the rest of the crew, Kemper included, but with considerably less skill than Grussmacher. No one had near the mechanical skills of Petry.

"The rest of us," Kemper said, "are going to explore these buildings. Gear up, including respirators and sidearms. Worona, status check?"

"Still a ways to go," the doctor replied. "So far, negative on anything harmful."

"Until you're certain, we'll remain on respirators."

"Aye, sir. I can stay behind and finish, if you want."

"Negative. Petry can continue the scans while we're gone."

The crew carried out his orders with their usual efficiency. Within minutes, he stood clustered together at the exit hatch with Shu, Grussmacher, and Worona. Kemper fitted a small, clear mask over his mouth and nose and activated the seal. The others followed suit. Once this was completed, Petry operated the hatch release. There was a metal clank, followed by a hiss and a rush of air.

Kemper breathed in. Beside him, the others did the same. No one spoke, but he knew they all had the same thought. More than two hundred billion humans had lived on planet Earth by the time they left; innumerably more in the millennia that followed. Yet, they were the first people ever to breathe air on an alien world, even if it was through a filter.

For the most part, the scent of the air was similar to that of their home planet. The only difference was that the atmosphere had a sharp metallic tint riding underneath. After a moment, Kemper lowered the automated ladder. Once it thudded into the ground, he climbed downward. Another first for mankind occurred as his boots thudded to the turf. He put the historic significance aside and glanced around. The ruins that surrounded them had a dusty hue to them, giving him the impression they had lain undisturbed for many years. As he moved away from the craft, he examined the broken pieces of the buildings more closely. The architecture looked both familiar and foreign, much like when he traveled from the western cities to those in Asia. The underlying framework was familiar, but the cosmetic appearance was different.

Shu joined him a few moments later. She followed his gaze. "Their constructions seem to be built based upon the circle," she said. Her hand swept toward the battered buildings before them. "And the oval."

"They appear to be crafted out of solid stone," Kemper noted.

"But not carved from natural occurrences," agreed Shu. "It's like they were able to work the stone into the desired shapes."

Kemper marveled at the technology while the remainder of the crew formed up next to him. Concrete was one thing—humans had been using various forms of that since the Romans, who had arguably been the best at it—but this was something beyond what they were capable of on Earth.

Or *were* capable of, when they left, Kemper reminded himself. There was no way to know his home civilization's present capabilities. For all he knew, engineers could also be morphing stone at will now.

Shu pointed at the grandest building, a few hundred meters away. "That could be some sort of government center," she said.

"What makes you say that? The size?"

"I'm guessing, really. So much of culture is a product of our own social construct that it is difficult to know if an alien culture adopted any similar constructs." Shu motioned to the city around them. "The fact that the Kyrans developed an urban environment like this greatly increases the likelihood we might share some commonalities, though. Like a city hall of sorts."

Kemper agreed and the five set off in that direction. In the distance, he spotted a flock of bird-like creatures moving across the sky. He pointed them out.

"Are they birds or bats?" Grussmacher asked.

Worona put her hand to her forehead to shield the sun. "Hard to say at this distance. They appear to be mostly gliding, though. I'm intrigued that a species on this planet developed flight, though."

"Not a common adaptation?" Shu asked her.

Worona shrugged, her eyes still tracking the tiny flock on the horizon. "How can we know? We only have one data point—Earth. However, seeing this is good evidence that it isn't uncommon."

"So it's good we came down to the surface, then?" Grussmacher teased blandly.

Worona smirked but conceded it was. She put a pair

of field glasses to her eyes and adjusted the instrument, then lowered them and shook her head. "Too far away to make out any detail." Even so, she stared after the flock longingly. "Fascinating, though."

Kemper waited a few more seconds to allow his biologist/doctor to contemplate the diminishing image of the flying birds or bats, then continued toward the main structure Shu had identified.

As they neared the front of the building, a battered and broken statue stood in front. Only the bottom portion of the figure's distinctly jointed Kyran legs remained on the pedestal, sheared off at an angle. A few readable glyphs adorned the front, making Kemper wish Shu had been able to translate the welcome message.

The anthropologist took a moment to photograph the statue and inscription. She glanced over at Kemper. "I wish Petry were here to take a look at the break points on this. Or the building damage, for that matter. I can't tell for certain if it's the result of time and nature or some kind of assault."

Kemper eyed the ragged stone that made up the top of the statue remains. He looked nearby for any semblance of what could have fallen over whenever it broke, and saw nothing but indistinguishable rock. "The rest of it looks to be gone," he said to Shu. "Carried off? By a conquering enemy, perhaps?"

Shu gently nudged some of the nearby rubble. "Or damaged by the elements." She pointed at the legs still on the plinth. "Even what remains standing has taken one hell of a beating."

"How long, do you think?" Kemper asked.

Shu pressed her lips together and shrugged. "That's what I'd like to hear from Petry. An engineer would have a better estimate than me. My focus isn't archeological."

"Guess," Kemper urged.

Shu reached out and fingered the stone on the pedestal. "Hundreds of years, Captain. At least."

"Great," muttered Grussmacher.

Kemper looked at the downward break atop what remained of the figure's legs. The stone was uneven, pitted. "Sliced, somehow?" he wondered aloud. "Or just the weak point in the manufacture?"

"You're thinking earthquake?" Shu asked, nodding her head in agreement.

"Or time," said Kemper. "Hundreds of years, right? I think back to the stone monuments of ancient Earth. Most are at least this damaged."

An image of his own house back on Earth sprang to Kemper's mind. He pushed the thought away. His home had a steward watching over it. No one was watching over these ruins.

"I hope that's the case," said Grussmacher. "I don't know that I'd want to come up against the weapon that could cleave stone like that."

"Me, either," Kemper muttered.

They turned away from the statue and mounted the wide, flat steps up to the building. Oval pillars had once stood to each side of what Kemper expected were the doors, but the pillars were badly shattered into pale remnants of what they had once been. He tried to envision them grandly rising up next to the opening. They must have been at least twenty meters high, he estimated.

Carefully, they picked their way through the rubble until Grussmacher found a path to the opening beyond. Kemper activated his flashlight and led the way.

Inside the building, the air was still and undisturbed. Swaths of light cut through the irregular holes in the ceiling, allowing him to see the general layout of the chamber within. There appeared to be no anterooms, just one single large area. The floor was uneven. Some of that came from whatever had caused all the damage—time, weather, war, Kemper remained unsure—and it was also clear there were several distinct levels within the massive room. Not enough of a difference between levels to signify multiple floors, as the rise was less than a meter.

He pointed it out to Shu.

"I noticed that," she said. "Again, it's pure speculation on my part but, if this was a gathering area, the different floor heights could be reserved for those of different status or rank."

"Social hierarchy, you mean? Or political?"

Shu nodded. "Or, if we compare it to our own early history, the division could be a caste system, perhaps delineated by race or species."

Kemper thought of the three different species of Kyrans depicted in the welcome message. Had the ones Shu called the elves held dominion over the dwarves and orcs? He supposed it was possible.

They wandered throughout the massive open hall. The only sounds were the amplified scrapes and crunches of their own footsteps. Meanwhile, Shu took extensive photos and video clips. At one point, she paused in front of a partially smashed relief on one wall. The carving depicted a Kyran of the elf species in formal attire. The top half was missing, giving the impression the figure had been slashed from shoulder to hip and the top portion had fallen away. The damage resembled the statue outside, though only generally. In the vast expanse of time, he conceded the probability of mere coincidence.

Shu searched the rubble on the ground nearby but found nothing in the battered pieces.

"Stolen or disintegrated?" Kemper wondered aloud.

Shu shrugged. "Depending on which, it tells a very different story, though, doesn't it?"

After an hour, they had made an entire circuit of the structure and returned to the entrance.

"What does this tell us?" Kemper asked Shu.

"That they were almost certainly a social civilization with a form of government," the anthropologist told him. "Whether it was secular or a form of theocracy, I can't determine. Most of whatever symbols they displayed are no longer intact, or even discernible. They appeared to have some sort of status system, possibly based upon species but, again, I can't say that for certain."

"No indications about what happened to them?"

Shu shook her head. "As we've discussed, it's impossible to tell whether all of this damage is due to time and natural phenomenon such as earthquakes or if it originated with some sort of warfare. If it was war, though, I stand by my earlier assessment; it happened a long time ago."

Kemper glanced around at the chamber and back to

the slashed or broken relief. "We've learned all we're going to in here," he said. "Let's move on."

The crew picked its way back through the entrance and to the steps. Kemper looked around at the other buildings. None were in better shape than this meeting hall, and all were notably smaller. Unless they were able to discover a subsurface level, it appeared to him that they were simply looking at a pile of rubble. He considered asking Shu which pile she wanted to examine next, but noticed the sun dipping low on the horizon.

"Let's check in with Achebe," he said. "Then we'll get a meal and a good night's sleep." He glanced at Shu. "Tomorrow, we'll split into groups and tackle whichever buildings you decide."

7

Achebe responded to Kemper's message with a terse "NTR."

Nothing to report.

Kemper found that comforting.

"We should have an old-fashioned campfire," Grussmacher said. Kemper couldn't tell if the pilot were joking or not as he motioned toward the sky. "Sleep under the strange Kyran stars."

Kemper wished they could, and perhaps they would, eventually. But protocol was clear—they'd spend the night inside the *Doncellita.*

The crew climbed into the small shuttle and Petry sealed the door.

Once the craft was closed up, the crew settled into their flight seats. Worona returned to scanning the atmosphere, taking over Petry's efforts the engineer had made in her absence. Kemper expected the engineer to pepper them with questions, but Petry was subdued and focused on the ship's status. When Shu filled him in on the broad strokes of their discovery, the dour Slav merely grunted and said, "War, sounds like. A violent species, just as I predicted."

Petry's dark mood seemed contagious as the team sat and ate a quiet meal, each lost in their own thoughts. For his part, Kemper ran the images of the nearly destroyed statue surrounded by the ruins of buildings past his mind's eye over and over again. Did some massive battle cause that damage, like Petry believed? Or was the Kyran fate something less self-destructive but every bit as fatal? If so, he and his team had merely observed what almost eight centuries of wear can do to a structure, even one made of stone.

"If it wasn't war," he murmured, almost to himself, "what was it?"

"Famine?" Grussmacher guessed.

Worona shook her head. "The existence of wildlife and flora doesn't tend to support that."

"Maybe the environment has recovered since it happened."

"Maybe," she allowed. "If I were betting, my money would be on some sort of pandemic. Something akin to the Bubonic Plague or The Spanish Flu. Wipes out the people and leaves behind the buildings."

"They aren't people," Petry said blandly.

Worona opened her mouth to reply, but Shu stepped in. "They're alien," she said, "that's true. But they're people, too."

"Besides," Worona added, "this is their planet. We're the aliens here."

Petry's only reply was a scowl.

"How do we know it's this way everywhere?"

Grussmacher asked. "Maybe this is just a wasteland and the populated area is just over the horizon."

"Always the optimist," teased Worona.

"Every pilot is an optimist," he said. "Trust me, you want us to be. Otherwise, we're flying on eggshells, and that's a recipe for disaster."

"He makes a good point," said Shu.

"About optimism?"

"About possibilities. So far, we haven't detected any sign of an existing civilization but our sensors aren't foolproof. There might be settlements or small towns we couldn't detect from orbit. The *Doncellita's* sensors are even more limited. We may yet discover what we came here to find. Perhaps tomorrow we'll come across something in the ruins that will point the way."

"Another optimist," said Worona.

"Every cosmic anthropologist is an optimist," Shu said slyly. "Trust me, you want us to be. Otherwise, we'd predict every first contact to be *War of the Worlds.*"

That brought out light laughter from the crew. Even Petry cracked a smile.

"All right," Kemper ordered, "Let's all try to get some rest."

"Do you want to set a guard?" Petry asked him.

Kemper shook his head. "That's the one advantage to not camping outside," he said. "Everyone can sleep at once."

Petry shrugged. His expression was well-known to Kemper now, as it conveyed the engineer knew the right—and only—answer to every one of life's puzzles, but all of the less enlightened people around him refused to see it.

Kemper closed his eyes. He spent a few moments considering the plan for the next day. Search the remaining nearby buildings, then back into the air to survey the surrounding area. He let himself feel mildly hopeful before drifting off into a soldier's sleep.

Almost five hours later, he was awoken by the *Doncellita* rocking violently, which set off the proximity alarm.

Kemper's eyes snapped open. He wondered briefly if he'd imagined the jerking motion of the craft, but there was no mistaking the gentle claxon of the proximity alarm. He opened his mouth to tell Grussmacher to disengage it when a chorus of terrible howls cut him off.

An electric chill coursed through him. He glanced at Shu, whose eyes were still befuddled by sleep. No help there, so he looked out the small cockpit window. There was nothing visible except inky blankness.

He waited for another round of howls but none came. Grussmacher started to speak, but Kemper held up his hand to stop him. He motioned for the pilot to reset the proximity alarm. Grussmacher punched a button and the light, urgent sound ceased. Kemper tensed, expecting it to go off again right away, but there was only silence. As the minutes passed, he made eye contact with each crew member. Sleep had fallen away and he was met with various mixes of concern and curiosity. Kemper breathed in and out, slowly and deeply, his ears piqued. The slightly metallic tang of the planet's atmosphere rested on his tongue.

After a while, he broke the silence in a quiet voice. "What the hell was that?"

"No way to know," Shu answered.

"Did anyone else feel the craft move?"

Shu shook her head, as did Petry, but Worona and Grussmacher both nodded firmly.

"So, whatever it was had to be a big enough creature to nudge the *Doncellita*," Kemper said.

"Or a large enough group to do so collectively," said Shu.

Kemper accepted the possibility of her theory with a nod. "Those howls were... a little unnerving," he admitted.

No one spoke but he saw agreement in their eyes.

"Could it have been one of the Kyran species?" he asked. "Was it an attack?"

The crew remained quiet. He noticed everyone else was looking to Shu for an answer, since this was her area of expertise.

The anthropologist spoke carefully. "That sound was the first vocalization we've heard since we landed. From any creature whatsoever. There's no baseline for me to judge. This could have easily been one of those herd animals we saw just outside the city."

"Those looked like herbivores," said Worona.

"Elephants are herbivores. One of them brushing up against the ship would move it like you described."

Kemper considered her point. "Those creatures looked docile," he said.

Shu turned over her hands. "Maybe, maybe not. Docile creatures can be curious. Many animals have a bark or cry far more fearsome than their actual disposition."

Petry shook his head. "So, you're saying we're dealing with a bunch of space cows who scream like banshees?"

"I'm not saying anything. I'm offering possibilities."

"One possibility," said Petry, "is that some kind of hostile creature—maybe the Kyrans—just attacked our ship."

"That is one possibility," Shu agreed.

"It's a disturbing one, don't you think?"

Before Shu could answer, Kemper intervened. "How long until dawn?" he asked Grussmacher.

The pilot consulted his instrumentation. "Three hours and sixteen minutes."

"Let's get some more sleep, then," Kemper told them. "I need each of you sharp come daylight."

He was met with dubious stares but no argument. As time passed, the crew members dozed, though Worona spent more time scanning the atmosphere outside. Eventually, she leaned back and closed her eyes. Kemper himself remained alert, running the problem through his mind. When sunlight finally peeked over the horizon and flooded through the cockpit window, he climbed out of his flight seat.

His action roused the remainder of the crew. Wordlessly, they geared up in the tight confines of the *Doncellita*. Once prepared, Kemper signaled Grussmacher to release the hatch. There was no rush of air this time, just the slightest hiss when the seal was broken.

Kemper lowered the hatchway ladder and climbed quickly downward. He immediately stepped to the side and drew his sidearm, scanning three-hundred-sixty degrees. The ruined cityscape that surrounded them was still. Kemper remained on guard until the rest of the crew had exited the craft. Then they fanned out, looking for any evidence to explain the previous night's events.

Worona scanned the ground. Kemper guessed she was looking for footprints or animal droppings that might support Shu's curious herbivore theory. He doubted the doctor would find prints on the broken, rocky ground, but some scat was always possible.

Kemper holstered his sidearm and wandered around the perimeter of the *Doncellita*, passing Petry in the process. The engineer was conducting a slow, methodical examination, as was his nature. Shu and Grussmacher faced outward, searching the ground and nearby landscape for any signs.

Three quarters of the way around the craft, Kemper stopped. Near the rear thruster, three jagged lines scored the hull. He stepped closer and examined the markings. They weren't deep, barely scratching the surface.

He called out to the crew, who gathered around and stared at the marking. Petry let out a low whistle when he saw the marks. "Given the metallurgical makeup of the *Doncellita*, whatever caused that had to be both sturdy and sharp."

"And wielded by someone of considerable strength," added Worona.

"A blade of some kind?" Kemper asked.

Shu peered more closely at the marks. "More likely

a claw," she said quietly. "Look at the spacing."

Petry muttered something inaudible.

Shu glanced at the pilot, then to Kemper. "It's still impossible to gauge aggressiveness, Captain. This could be a docile, curious creature unaware of its own strength."

"Or a predator," Petry said. "Some giant bear or whatever."

Shu tilted her head, then gave a short nod. "That is just as possible."

"Stay aware," Kemper ordered. "Keep your weapons handy. We'll all stay together today, Petry included. No separate groups as previously planned."

Together, the crew picked their way toward the first building Shu selected. It was considerably smaller than the main hall they'd explored yesterday but still impressive. The front entrance was impassable but Grussmacher located a secondary entrance through what seemed to Kemper like a window.

Inside, the floor was littered with more than just rubble. Scattered pieces of technology were also strewn among the stones. Petry examined these broken components and proclaimed them as "part of some kind of computer," although he couldn't determine how they functioned, since they appeared to be mostly stone as well. Only a fine inlay of spidery metal fibers differentiated it from the nearby rubble.

The Kyrans, it seemed to Kemper, had developed technology to work stone in a manner similar to how metal was manipulated on Earth. This was a fascinating find and one that would have intrigued Kemper more if it weren't for the tension from the night visitor hanging over them.

They managed to explore the remains of several other buildings throughout the day. One appeared to be for residential use while the purpose of others was difficult to determine. Shu was thoroughly engrossed in the process but Kemper noticed the remainder of the crew, particularly Grussmacher, spent at least as much time on guard against an attack as searching the ruins.

Kemper shared the pilot's concern. The shadow of potential danger enveloped him as he trailed Shu from building to building.

Near the end of the day, they reassembled at the *Doncellita*. While they stood near the footings of the shuttle and ate, Kemper asked the crew for a recommendation for their next action.

"Return to altitude and continue to search for civilization," Petry said immediately.

Kemper glanced at Shu. "You agree?"

Shu nodded. "After all," she said, "ruins exist on Earth, too. As we discussed last night, that doesn't mean there aren't populated cities, or at least settlements of some kind elsewhere on the planet."

Grussmacher was less convinced but didn't outright disagree. "It'd be nice to find hard evidence as to what happened to them," the pilot said. "Whether it was plague or war or some kind of mass exodus."

Kemper concurred. "Let's get started immediately," he ordered.

The crew finished eating and boarded the *Doncellita,* strapping in. Once the craft was airborne, Kemper ordered Grussmacher to resume a flight path at fifteen hundred meters. "Worona will scan," he said, "while Petry and Shu sleep. In four hours, you'll swap roles."

"You need sleep, too, Captain," Worona told him.

Kemper gave her an indulgent smile. "Yes, Doctor." Somehow, he thought he might sleep more peaceably in the air than sitting on the ground.

Grussmacher chose a heading that took the *Doncellita* overland, though Kemper was beginning to wonder if they'd need to figure out a way to search the oceans, as well. He put that consideration aside for now. He made radio contact with Achebe to ensure everything was status quo aboard the *Doncella*. Once again, Achebe's terse reply was "NTR." After last night's possible attack, Kemper found that comforting once more. He acknowledged the message, waited until Petry and Shu had fallen asleep, and finally closed his own eyes as well.

He awoke to a gentle beeping.

For a brief moment, he flashed back to coming out of cryo aboard the *Doncella*. His disorientation quickly faded, however, and he glanced toward Grussmacher.

"What is it?" he asked sleepily, rubbing his eyes.

Petry and Shu were still asleep, so Kemper assumed he'd only been out for a couple of hours. Grussmacher didn't reply to him, as the pilot was focused on his instruments.

Worona gave him an excited look. "We're looping back around on a less developed settlement."

Kemper cocked his head. "Less developed?"

"A tribal village, from the looks of it," Worona clarified. "Just like on our planet, it's entirely possible for one species to have various civilizations at different levels of technological development."

"I realize that," Kemper said, keeping the irritation out of his tone. "But the mission is to allot our limited research resources to the apex civilization, at least at first. Why are we investigating this one?"

"Shu has a theory."

Kemper glanced at the sleeping woman. "What theory?"

"She believes it is most likely the Kyrans experienced an existential event, likely self-induced, that shattered their civilization. If this happened hundreds of years ago, the ensuing result to those who remained would be a form of technological regression."

"They bombed themselves back to the Stone age?" Kemper asked, recalling a famous statement from somewhere in history.

"Essentially. Though, to which age of development they currently reside within remains to be seen."

Kemper considered the theory. All they had seen of any civilization thus far were ruins. Not recent destruction, either, but ruins easily decades old, more likely hundreds of years. Shu's theory fit on that count.

Then something else occurred to him. "When did Shu share this theory with you? I haven't heard it yet."

Worona smiled at him. "While you slept, Captain."

Kemper furrowed his brow in confusion. Then he called up the chronometer and noted the time. He'd been asleep for almost nine hours, long enough for the crew to cycle through an entire shift change.

"Why didn't anyone wake me?"

"Doctor's orders," said Worona. "You needed rest."

He opened his mouth to protest but stopped himself. Worona's duties included looking after the physical and mental health of the crew. That included him. As much as he didn't like the idea of sleeping while his crew worked, he knew her judgment was sound.

"I have further good news," Worona reported. "Petry and I have completed our analysis of the atmosphere."

"Did you detect anything that merits continued use of respirators?"

Worona hesitated. "Understand that we can't predict how our biology will interact with every—"

"Doctor," Kemper interrupted gently. "I realize that even on earth, virology is situation dependent. All I want to know is if you're confident that without respirators, we are at least as safe as a foreigner in a new land."

The doctor nodded slowly. "I think that is a fair analogy. There is always a danger, but..."

"Wake the others," he ordered. "Let's see what this settlement has to offer."

8

At Kemper's direction, they set the ship down a kilometer from the settlement. Grussmacher found a small clearing atop a gentle rise and landed. The crew geared up wordlessly. When they'd finished, Kemper told Petry to remain with the *Doncellita.*

The engineer frowned at the order. Kemper thought he might voice his disagreement but, after a moment of consideration, Petry didn't argue. Instead, while the rest of the crew descended through the hatchway ladder, he went to his station and returned with a digital compass he held out to Kemper.

"It took a while to sync it to this planet's magnetic field, but I finally figured it out," Petry told him.

"Of course, you did," said Kemper, accepting the device. "Thanks."

Petry grunted something unintelligible and stepped back.

Kemper climbed down to where Worona, Grussmacher, and Shu waited. The four of them set off in the direction of the village, Kemper in the lead. The short hike wound through heavily wooded terrain. Kemper referenced the compass several times to ensure he maintained course, but each time his sense of direction was arrow straight.

After roughly a kilometer, the forest thinned and then opened up into a natural clearing. Kemper saw more than a dozen large huts, seemingly made of a mixture of wood, grass, and mud. Despite the crude materials, the craftsmanship was excellent.

A slender, lazy tendril of smoke rose from a central fire that had very nearly gone out, though whether it had been stamped upon in haste or merely burned itself down was unclear.

The light chatter of wildlife that had followed them on the short walk through the woods remained but the village itself was otherwise devoid of sound or movement. Kemper and the crew cautiously made their way toward the center of the village, peeking into a few of the huts as they passed.

All were empty.

"Where is everyone?" Kemper asked.

"Said Fermi," Shu joked tonelessly. Then she drew in a sharp breath.

"What is it?" Kemper asked. Shu's expression was difficult to decipher. Shocked, certainly. But he also saw exuberance. Kemper followed her gaze, turning toward what she'd seen.

In front of one of the huts, near the end of the row, sat a Kyran.

Grussmacher immediately drew his sidearm.

"Easy," Kemper said, holding out his hand toward

the pilot. "Put that away."

Grussmacher reluctantly obeyed.

"But... keep it handy," Kemper added. He glanced back at the Kyran who resembled one of the tall species Shu had labeled as Elves. Kemper turned to her now. "Doctor, I do believe this is your moment."

Shu shook her head. "You're the captain. It's for you to make first contact. I can take over from there, but the very first moment is supposed to be you."

Kemper didn't argue. He walked forward slowly, trying to project a peaceful intent. Of course, he knew body language differed between cultures within his own species. How many significant differences would there be between his species and an alien one?

The Kyran did not move. As he drew closer, he saw how the creature sat on folded legs with multiple joints, looking as if it could spring to its feet in a moment. The large, dark eyes regarded him without inflection. The gill-like feature was open and the light gray cilia twitched inquisitively.

He stopped at what he guessed was a prudent distance.

The Kyran stared at him, unmoving.

Kemper was about to ask Shu for some advice when he recalled the message they'd intercepted upon arriving in the solar system. He approximated the gesture with his right arm, angling it across his chest, keeping his hand open to project friendliness.

"Greetings," he said. The words felt inadequate, so he added, "We are honored to meet you."

The Kyran did not move but the hair-like tendrils of

its gills fluttered rapidly.

Kemper waited, holding his pose.

A broken, high pitched squeak emanated from the Kyran's mouth. The sound startled Kemper, despite the fact he'd been hoping for a reply. It went on for almost ten seconds, ranging in pitch and punctuated with brief silences.

Kemper forced himself to smile and nod. "Thank you for communicating with us," he said, doubting the Kyran understood. He turned to Shu. "Doctor?"

Shu looked up from her device. "Definitely a language pattern, sir."

"Any chance you can translate?"

"Eventually," she said. "But it'll take significant time."

"What about the silence? Is that part of the language?"

"Yes and no. Some of the silences you heard were just that—the lack of vocalization. But in at least one instance, his mouth continued to move during the silence. I believe those sounds were simply outside our auditory range."

Kemper nodded. He turned back to the Kyran, who was still watching him with those large dull eyes.

"I guess we're playing charades, then," he murmured.

No one answered.

Kemper lowered his arm. Then slowly, he pointed toward the empty huts throughout the village, one at a time. Then he made a circling gesture to signal all of them together, followed by a single motion away from the village. Then he turned up both hands questioningly.

The Kyran stared back at him.

"Do you think he understands?" Kemper asked Shu.

"You're asking where all his people are, correct?"

"Wasn't it obvious?" If his own crew couldn't understand his meaning, what chance did an alien species have?

"Yes, sir. To us. But body language is unlikely to translate directly. Even between cultures on our own—"

"They're a carbon-based, bipedal race of intelligent creatures on an Earth-like planet," Kemper said. "Some things have *got* to be universal."

Shu pressed her lips together. "Perhaps."

Kemper stepped slowly backward and to the side. As he did so, he swept his arms toward Shu, presenting her to the Kyran. The creature's head shifted slightly and it focused on the anthropologist.

Shu took several small steps forward. Then she lowered herself into a seated position, doing her best to approximate the Kyran's pose despite their anatomical differences.

She began to communicate.

Kemper watched with rapt fascination for almost an hour. But Shu's efforts moved at glacial speed, and he noted the sun was already descending toward the tops of the trees on the edge of the village glade.

"Stay with Shu," he directed Worona. As a biologist, she was the next best option to observe and learn about the Kyran. Her discipline was also best suited to taking scientific notes.

He motioned to Grussmacher. "You're with me."

Moving slowly so as not to startle the Kyran, he and the pilot began a methodical search of the village. They avoided going inside the huts, unsure how the Kyran might react, but they looked into each one.

The structures were simply furnished with tables and beds—Kemper saw no chairs—as well as some form of pottery. There were no other Kyrans to be seen. Grussmacher pointed out multiple instances of footprints in the softer earth on the fringes of the more well-trodden walkways. Kemper stared down at the markings that looked like they'd been left by a cross between a bird and a horse.

All around the edges of the village, they found these prints. A rough count, probably low, told Kemper that more than thirty Kyrans had fled the village.

"When you flew over, what was your altitude?" he asked Grussmacher.

"Same as before. Fifteen hundred meters."

"So they heard our engines."

"Most likely."

"And saw our ship."

"It would have been the size of a large bird to their eye, but yes."

"Their scouts probably saw us land, too," Kemper muttered. "I should have landed us five to ten kilometers away instead. Might not have scared off the population that way."

Grussmacher shrugged. "I like knowing the

Doncellita is only one klick away."

Kemper couldn't argue that.

They continued their search of the village. When they neared the largest hut, sudden frantic screeches stopped them. Kemper turned to see the Kyran had stood. At its full height, the alien looked to be over seven feet tall. It extended one thin arm toward them, as if pointing.

"Don't go in there," Shu called out to him.

"No kidding," Kemper said.

Carefully, he backed away. Without being told, Grussmacher did the same.

"Temple?" he asked Shu.

"That's a good guess."

Kemper walked back to where Shu stood with the Kyran. He mimed the greeting sign again, and bowed slightly.

The Kyran didn't return the gesture, but it did lower itself to a seated position once more. Kemper marveled at how gracefully the Kyran's legs folded together.

"It looks like the population fled," he told Shu and Worona. "Probably when they saw our ship."

"Makes sense," said Shu.

"Any progress?" he asked her.

"It's slow. But... I get the sense this is an elder. See how the skin is mottled and wrinkled in places?"

Kemper examined the Kyran closely. He saw a trace of mottling and the slightest evidence of wrinkles. All the while, the Kyran stared back at him with its large eyes.

"Is it making an effort to communicate?" he asked Shu.

"Yes."

"Well, keep at it, then."

Kemper and Grussmacher stood guard while Shu tried to learn how to converse with the Kyran. Worona observed and made notes.

After his own clumsy attempts at communication, Kemper admired the varied methods Shu used in order to achieve understanding. She employed body postures, gestures, symbols and math equations scratched in the ground, and words in a variety of Earth languages. She even attempted to approximate the Kyran squeaks. To Kemper's non-linguistic ear, she landed close on several of them.

Time passed. Kemper noticed the Kyran seemed to gradually become more engaged with Shu, though the creature's motions and vocalizations were still infrequent. Shu's assessment that the process would be slow seemed an understatement.

Kemper kept an eye on the sun as it dipped below the tree line. He estimated perhaps an hour until darkness fell. He had a decision to make.

"Shu?" he asked gently.

"Sir?"

"Are you getting anywhere?"

"A watched pot never boils, sir."

"Maybe not, but it's going to get dark soon. I have to decide whether we stay or head back to the *Doncellita*. So I need to know if you have any momentum or if you want to start again in the morning."

Shu hesitated. Then she said, "I'd like to keep at it, sir."

Kemper considered. He glanced around the empty village. The Kyrans had lived here for some time. They likely fled because of the ship, not any natural predators. If they could be safe here, perhaps the crew could be as well.

It was a risk, he knew. The safest bet was to spend the night inside the comparatively safe confines of the *Doncellita*. Then again, in his long career, he'd learned to trust the judgment of his crew, especially when it came to their area of expertise.

"We'll stay here," he announced. Then he waved for Grussmacher to follow him. The two gathered wood and returned to the village center. After dumping an armload each near the smoldering fire, he looked toward the Kyran and motioned for permission. The Kyran didn't respond. Considering how it had reacted to them when they got too close to the temple, he took this silence as acquiescence. Stacking the wood carefully atop the dying embers, he blew on them until the flames kicked up and licked at the new wood. Soon the fire was alive and crackling. Kemper held his hands out to the warmth.

"Contact Petry," he directed Grussmacher. "Let him know we're staying here."

Grussmacher stepped away, raising his portable radio to his lips. Meanwhile Kemper positioned himself so he could watch Shu and the Kyran. He and Grussmacher would have to share the guard duties throughout the night, he realized. Shu's efforts were of primary mission importance at the moment and

Worona's assistance and note-taking almost as crucial. With the prospect of a long night ahead, he was suddenly glad they'd let him sleep during the search earlier.

Dusk set in. Shu continued to work with the Kyran. Kemper couldn't tell if the creature's focus was solely on the anthropologist or if it watched all of them. At times, it sat preternaturally still, staring blankly, reminding Kemper of a meditating monk. Only the occasional gesture or squeak punctuated these long moments of inaction.

Kemper put another log on the fire. He made a rough calculation and decided they might need more wood. He told Grussmacher to remain on guard while he walked toward the tree line. He listened carefully while he walked. The sounds of the Kyran daytime had faded as the light dimmed and the air cooled. A chorus of new sounds replaced the old. Kemper heard the light hum of insects and the strangled coo of a bird.

He flicked on his personal light, setting the intensity just high enough for him to avoid tripping over logs or rocks. Gathering the wood took much longer than in the daylight. Kemper kept his ears piqued as he picked up each piece. After a while, he'd filled his arms and started back toward the clearing.

Behind him, the distinct crack of a large twig snapping reverberated through the woods.

Kemper froze.

The insect hum remained but the pained coos from the bird stopped abruptly. Kemper stood motionless for almost a minute, straining his hearing to pick up any other sounds. In the distance, he heard the crackle of the village fire and Shu's occasional vocalization, but nothing else.

Something broke that branch, he told himself.

He recalled all of the herd animals they'd seen so far. Clearly, the fauna on Kyra-2B had sufficient size to have made that noise. If the creature had subsequently sensed him after making the sound, it would have frozen in place as well. Especially if it were prey.

A predator would do the same.

Kemper started moving again. He picked his way along slowly, trying to make as little noise as possible and listening the entire while. He heard no other telltale signs of movement. He noticed the cooing of the bird did not return, either.

Once in the clearing, he strode directly toward the fire and added his armload of wood to the pile. He found Grussmacher and spoke in a low voice.

"Something's out there."

"I imagine quite a few somethings," Grussmacher said humorlessly. "Let's hope they're either friendly or scared of us. Or fire."

"Let's hope," Kemper agreed.

A few hours passed.

Kemper thought the Kyran grew slightly but steadily more engaged with Shu, but he couldn't be entirely certain. For her part, Shu was tireless, moving from one effort to another without a shred of apparent frustration.

"Get some rest," Kemper ordered Grussmacher.

"I can power through," the pilot said, but Kemper

could see the exhaustion in the man's face.

"No need. I'll wake you after a few hours. Sleep."

Reluctantly, Grussmacher leaned against the outside of the hut nearest the fire. He crossed his arms and let his chin come to his chest. Within minutes, he was asleep.

Kemper kept the fire fed, though he let it diminish to a lower burn level in order to conserve fuel. He took a food ration from his day pack and ate slowly while he scanned the perimeter of the village. The flickering light from the campfire created shadows that danced and leapt across the trees and bushes, playing tricks on his eyes. He watched for any eyes peering out of the woods, wondering if there were any animals on Kyra-2B that had reflective lenses like some did on Earth.

He kept his back to the fire as much as possible to conserve some remnant of his vision in the dark. The cool air of night closed in on the front of him while the fire kept his back warm. The strange duality seemed somehow fitting for the overwhelmingly surreal nature of the reality he was experiencing.

I am standing on a planet not my own, he thought, *guarding against unknown species, while my crew member communicates with an alien life form.*

Given the many vagaries of space exploration, the sheer volume of what could go wrong, he had to admit, if this was the only contact they made throughout the entire mission, the scientists would still deem the mission a massive success. Not to mention the prospect of another planet capable of sustaining human life. The CSA would be thrilled about this fact alone.

If the CSA even exists anymore.

Kemper pushed away the thought, saving it for another day. He added another branch to the fire, kicking up sparks. The Kyran, who had been silent for some time, let out a broken squeak. When he looked over, all three beings were staring out into the darkness. He realized suddenly that all of the night sounds from the woods had ceased.

Then he saw the eyes.

At first glance, he counted perhaps a dozen pairs, sprinkled amongst the trees. They shone with a feral yellow, reflecting back the firelight.

He raised his pistol automatically. "Gruss," he said, his tone low and urgent.

Grussmacher roused from sleep and scrambled to his feet. He didn't have to be told where to look, keying immediately on the surrounding eyes. The pilot muttered a curse and leveled his sidearm toward the trees.

Worona broke away from the palaver and joined them near the fire. The doctor kept her weapon holstered, but she broke the strap away with her thumb for easy access. No one spoke. The yellow eyes watched them without blinking. Neither Shu nor the Kyran made any noise or moved.

Fifteen long minutes passed. Then twenty. Kemper slowly lowered his weapon but kept it drawn. Grussmacher mirrored his action. Sweat streamed down Kemper's neck and trunk, but his skin prickled with cold anticipation.

Then, suddenly, one of the sets of eyes disappeared.

There came the slight sound of rustling, barely discernible. After that, the remaining eyes blinked out in quick succession. A whisper of movement followed, and they were gone.

The crew waited, expecting the creatures to reappear. Another half hour passed but there were no more eyes. The ambient night sounds slowly returned to the surrounding forest.

"Anyone get a look at their bodies?" Kemper asked quietly.

"Negative," came the replies.

"So, we have no idea how big a creature those eyes belonged to," he mused. He glanced at Worona for her biology expertise. "Any estimate?"

"The potential is wide-ranging," she replied.

"Best guess."

"At least our size. But the possibility exists that they are considerably larger."

"Not prey animals," Kemper said, more of a statement than a question. "Predators."

"Perhaps. They could be a variety of scavengers. Like coyotes on Earth, for example. Curious enough to check us out, to look for vulnerabilities. Since we didn't look like easy pickings, they moved on."

"Or went for reinforcements," said Grussmacher.

Worona shrugged, acknowledging the possibility.

Kemper scanned the tree line, seeing nothing. He directed Worona to return to assisting Shu while he and Grussmacher resumed guard duty.

"You should get some rest, too, Captain," Grussmacher said.

"I'm good."

"We need you at your best, sir, just like the rest of us." Grussmacher hefted his pistol. "I've got this."

Kemper hesitated. Then he said, "Wake me if the eyes return."

"Of course."

He wandered closer to Shu and Worona. "Any progress?"

"Baby steps," Worona called to him.

"Keep at it, but break to rest if you need it."

"Aye, sir."

He considered what they might do at first light. Continue the attempts to communicate? Regroup at the *Doncellita*? He decided he'd make that determination once the sun rose and he'd reached that particular decision point.

Reluctantly, Kemper settled into the same location Grussmacher had used, pressing his back against the side of a hut. He didn't think he'd be able to fall asleep after having seen the appraising yellow eyes in the dark forest but, after a short while, he drifted off.

9

He woke to chaos.

Shouts.

A strangled shriek he realized came from the Kyran.

Two quick bursts from a nearby gun.

Kemper scrambled to his feet. The night closed in on him as he drew his weapon. The fire had burned down to its embers, a muted orange glow that barely cast shadows of the crew members huddled near it.

Other shadows drew his attention. Flashes of frantic movement slipping through the village. A dark silhouette stood near the fire, shooting into the darkness.

Grussmacher.

Another shriek.

Kemper wheeled toward it. An explosion of light and then the concussive sound of a gun came from the direction of the Kyran elder, where Worona and Shu had been. In the brief moment of illumination, he saw a still shot of the Kyran and Worona both lying on the ground at Shu's feet. Shu wielded her weapon, leveling it at an oncoming creature. A stocky bipedal outstretched its arms toward Shu, its teeth bared and slavering.

Kemper took a step in that direction, calling out to them.

Another blast, another freeze frame. The attacking creature falling away from Shu, wounded.

More blasts from Grussmacher.

Kemper grabbed a chunk of wood and threw it onto the fire, then charged toward Shu. In the darkness, he could see their shapes, fuzzy and indistinct. Shu dragged Worona along the ground with one arm. Her weapon was up defensively in her strong hand.

"Friendly behind!" shouted Kemper, so she didn't wheel around and shoot him. "I've got her!"

Without looking his way, Shu let go of Worona's still form. She brought her free hand up to steady her weapon and kept her attention trained outward.

Kemper holstered, knelt, and flung Worona over his shoulder. As he rose, he heard more shots from Grussmacher. He adjusted the weight, shifting it so he could draw his own pistol again.

"Retreat toward the fire," he ordered.

He and Shu shuffled backward toward the fire's glow which had kicked up with small flames from the log Kemper had added. The light brightened and extended outward. Kemper saw the dark gray skin of their attackers, their thick bodies, the glint of their clawed thumb. They shifted and moved, at least a half dozen of them, as if trying to dodge their way out of the light.

Grussmacher's shooting stopped abruptly. The pilot let out a painful groan. Before Kemper could turn to see what happened, the shots resumed, along with a string of virulent curses.

He and Shu kept moving backward. The closer he got to the fire, the more the creatures backed away, eventually melting into the trees again, until all he could see were the now-familiar feral yellow eyes glaring out at them.

Kemper lowered the unconscious Worona to the ground and scanned for enemies. "More wood," he ordered Shu. "Get a roaring blaze going."

Shu holstered and obeyed. She stacked several logs onto the fire, then knelt beside Worona as the flames leapt upward.

"She still with us?" Kemper asked, keeping his eyes on the staring yellow eyes.

"Barely."

"Do what you can." He glanced over at Grussmacher, whose right arm dangled at his side. Dark blood dripped from his fingers. The pilot's pistol extended outward in his left hand, and he shifted through his targets methodically as if being in his sights was what kept the creatures at bay.

Several feet away, a thick gray body lay crumpled to the ground.

One of Shu's orcs. The third Kyran species.

Grussmacher let loose another blast. The round crashed through the brush near the clump of eyes. Several blinked out. A moment later, the rest shifted away.

Kemper stood at the ready while Shu tended to Worona. His gaze scanned the wooded area for eyes while he strained his ears to hear any movement. After a while, Shu rose from tending Worona to bind the gash on Grussmacher's bicep.

"How bad?" Kemper asked Shu.

"I'm fine," Grussmacher grunted before she could reply. "A glancing blow."

"From a weapon?"

Grussmacher shook his head while Shu finished tying the bandage. "Claw. I pulled back at the last second. Escaped the worst of it."

Kemper nodded his understanding, then looked to Shu. "And Worona?"

"I saw her take a blow to the head. There are also some slashes across her chest, but I think the worst injury is a puncture wound to her abdomen. I stopped any external bleeding, but I can't know for sure if she's bleeding internally or not."

Kemper considered the situation. After Worona, Achebe had the most medical cross-training. The medical facilities on the *Doncella* were superior to what they had at their disposal here. That made his decision regarding what to do at first light much easier. He needed to get Worona back to the mother ship.

First, though, they had to make it through the night.

The three crew members all stood with their backs to the fire, each covering a different zone of darkness beyond what the flickering flames illuminated. Kemper kept the fire stoked high, grateful for the extra wood they'd collected earlier. He glanced toward the hut where the elder Kyran had been sitting, but saw nothing.

"Did it run into the hut?" he asked Shu.

The anthropologist shook her head sadly. "The first creature that attacked went for the elder right away. Sunk his claws in and tore..." She trailed off. "It threw the elder to the side. Beside the hut, I think. I'm not sure. By then, another one of the creatures was attacking Worona."

"I'm sorry," Kemper told her.

Grimly, Shu dipped her chin. Clearly, mourning any new friends would have to wait. He admired her resolve.

Kemper turned back to his quadrant. He didn't look at Grussmacher directly, but asked, "Why'd you let the fire burn so low?"

"To conserve wood," Grussmacher answered. Before Kemper could respond, the pilot added, "I miscalculated, Captain. The attack was my fault."

"No, it wasn't." Kemper shook his head. Letting the fire burn low might have encouraged the attackers but, given the savagery he saw in their brief battle, he strongly suspected an attack was inevitable. "Not entirely, at least."

Grussmacher didn't answer him.

Kemper lifted his radio to his lips and tried to raise Petry at the *Doncellita*.

There was no response.

He checked the device status and confirmed it was working. Pressing his lips together, he called again.

Still no answer.

"He may have shut things down to sleep," Shu suggested.

Grussmacher snorted, though his voice carried an underlying sense of worry. "Even if he did, he'd still leave the radio volume cranked to wake him."

"Maybe," said Shu, her tone hopeful but unconvinced. "He could just be sleeping hard. Or forgot to turn up the volume."

Kemper didn't reply. He kept the radio near, in case Petry initiated contact. Then, along with the other two, he watched, and waited.

As the first pale band of light brimmed the horizon, Kemper rubbed at his sleep-itchy eyes. He wondered if the daytime would be safe. Were the attackers nocturnal, put off by the light the fire cast or was it any kind of light that repelled them? If the flames were what gave them pause and they attacked in daylight, would the fire seem as potent to them as it did at night?

By the time the sun itself came into full view, he turned his thoughts to more immediate matters. Now that they'd survived the night, he re-prioritized his goals in order of exigency.

Ensure the injuries to Worona and Grussmacher were stabilized.

Get to the *Doncellita.*

Take off and return to the *Doncella,* where Worona could be more fully treated.

Re-evaluate the mission.

Nearby, Grussmacher used his foot to roll the thick body of one of the dead creatures onto its back. The pilot stared down at the alien corpse, his weapons still drawn and at his side. Kemper followed his gaze.

The Kyran resembled the orc species, to use Shu's earlier shorthand. It certainly fit that description, especially when compared to the more elegant creature she'd been trying to communicate with earlier. The creature's glazed eyes were smaller and more forward facing. The bright, menacing yellow in them made Kemper uncomfortable despite knowing the creature was dead. The mouth was larger than he remembered from the first message they saw upon entering the Kyran system; the teeth were sharper and more prevalent. The thumb claw at the end of its muscled arm looked like a pearl-colored hunting knife.

"They've regressed," Shu said quietly at his side.

Grussmacher scoffed. "They've become more efficient predators, you mean."

"Yes," Shu said. "They've begun to evolve away from civilization."

"There hasn't been time for that," said Grussmacher.

"A thousand years?" Shu asked. She glanced at Worona, as if wishing the biologist could weigh in. "What is that, almost two hundred generations? Think of the changes in our own species over that time period."

"We don't know their life span," Grussmacher said, but with little conviction in his voice.

"Even so, they've evolved since sending that welcome message into space." Shu pointed at the teeth Kemper had noticed before as proof. "Those developed because whatever broke the apex culture," she motioned toward the crumpled form of the Kyran she'd been attempting to communicate with, "took everyone back to a more basic time. A time in which the most efficient tools were no longer technology and intelligence, but those of a more savage and immediate variety." She glanced up. "It's amazing, in one sense. Over the course of centuries, a species already showing definitive signs of rapid adaptation to the changed environment... very resilient."

"I'm glad you admire them so much," Grussmacher snapped. "They only tried to slaughter us last night."

"To them," Shu said, "we are invaders."

"Is that what he said?" Kemper asked. He lifted his chin toward the fallen elf Kyran.

"I'm not certain *he* is the most accurate pronoun," said Shu.

"A female elder, then?"

Shu shook her head. "I may be wrong but I don't think they have a biological sex. Or, rather, each individual carries the capability to fulfill the role of either male or female for reproductive purposes. That was what Worona, thought, anyway."

"You got all that from your friend?" Kemper was impressed. He thought the progress had been going significantly slower.

"Not for certain. It only took hopping across a few logical lily pads to get to that concept." Shu knelt to check on the still unconscious Worona. "It does seem the Kyrans are asexual. They give birth to multiple young but die in the process."

"This is fascinating and all," Grussmacher interjected, "but I think our mission has devolved to survival level considerations. Don't you, Captain?"

Kemper nodded. "The two aren't necessarily mutually exclusive." He motioned for Shu to continue.

"Did you get anything else of importance? Anything we can use?"

Shu shook her head. "Like I said, even what I just shared is speculative. Truth be told, there was only one implication I feel certain about, because it was one they kept returning to."

"What was it?"

Shu glanced down at the dead orcish Kyran before answering. "That the coming of these predators was our fault. We brought them here, simply by our arrival."

10

They trudged back toward the *Doncellita.*

Kemper carried Worona draped over his shoulder. He was flanked by Shu and Grussmacher, both of whom walked with their weapons drawn. Grussmacher made several attempts to raise Petry on the radio. The pilot's voice was laced with frustration when there was no response.

Despite Worona's slight frame, Kemper's muscles soon burned underneath the weight. Breathing heavily, he kept moving through the trees, watching for the flitting forms of the orcish Kyrans and hoping the crew would reach the clearing ahead. He listened for crashing movement in the forest, but all he heard were the crew's own thudding steps.

By the time the shuttle came into sight, he was gasping for breath and his legs were leaden.

"Petry!" called Grussmacher as he trotted up the gradual incline toward the shuttle. "Prep for launch!"

There was no answer.

As Kemper approached the craft, he saw the open

hatchway on the underside. Bloody, viscous entrails hung from the edges of the entry.

"Oh, no," Shu breathed.

Kemper lowered Worona to the ground and drew his weapon. "Stay with her," he instructed Grussmacher. "And watch the tree line."

The pilot set his jaw and nodded.

Together with Shu, Kemper walked cautiously to the underside of the *Doncellita*. From directly beneath the hatch, he saw the ragged, torn torso protruding just past the edge.

Petry.

"Son of a bitch," muttered Kemper.

He activated the re-entry ladder remotely. The automated device started downward, then faltered, groaned, jerked, and stopped entirely. Kemper jumped up to grab it. He was able to pull himself up and then climb several rungs going hand over hand. Once he got his foot into the bottom-most rung, the rest of the short climb was easy.

Inside the shuttle, he saw the rest of Petry's upper body. The engineer was on his back, both arms splayed out to the sides. He stared dully up toward the ceiling with frozen, glazed eyes.

Kemper swept through the craft. He saw some surface damage—slash marks on the walls and some equipment—but wouldn't know if any crucial systems were compromised until they brought the ship online.

That would have to wait, however—they had something else to do first.

Gently, Kemper lowered Petry's body through the

hatch. Shu received it and moved it out from under the *Doncellita*. The engineer's lower half wasn't on board, so Kemper dropped out of the ship again and searched nearby. He found a blood trail leading away from the ship and followed it to the edge of the clearing.

Nothing.

He made a slow circle around the perimeter. Three quarters of the way around, he found the torn remnants of Petry's trunk and legs. Wordlessly, he lifted the grisly remains and carried them to where the engineer's torso rested. He lay the severed piece into place, giving Petry some semblance of wholeness again. Kemper took a moment to stare down at the still body. It occurred to him how much force it would take—and how sharp an implement—to cut a human body fully in half. A memory of the slashes to the exterior of the *Doncellita* sprang to his mind, followed by images of the powerful forms of their attackers from the previous night.

Kemper returned to the shuttle. It took him a few moments to remember where the Anytool was stored, but he found it. A few adjustments and snaps into position later, he had the makeshift shovel.

"There's no time for that," Grussmacher said. "You need to lift off and get back to the *Doncella* before those yellow-eyed bastards come back again."

"I'm not leaving him exposed to the elements," said Kemper.

"We're exposed here, Captain. If they attack—"

Kemper cut him off. "They're nocturnal." He glanced down at Worona's unconscious form, wishing for her expertise to confirm his theory. "They'll wait until dark."

Grussmacher pressed his lips together, the doubt on his face plain to see.

"He was part of our crew," Kemper insisted. "We're going to do right by him."

Grussmacher didn't reply.

They chose a place not far from the ship. Kemper dug in silence while Shu stood nearby, scanning the trees for more attackers. Grussmacher brought Worona over and laid her gently on the ground, then went inside the *Doncellita* to perform diagnostics. Shu knelt next to Worona, examining her while looking up intermittently to guard against attack.

"How is she?" he grunted, pausing to wipe away the sweat pouring into his eyes.

"Critical but stable," said Shu. "I don't see any signs of internal bleeding, but medicine is not my expertise. In any event, there is nothing more we can do for her until we reach the *Doncella.*"

Kemper dipped his chin in acknowledgment and resumed digging.

He'd experienced loss in service before. Holly, of course. Another time, an entire squad had perished on a spacewalk repair when a lifeline snapped, struck by unexpected space debris, sending them floating away one by one, pulled toward the nearby gravity well and dashed against the surface of one of Jupiter's moons. On Mars, one of his soldiers fell off a small cliff, shattering his tibia. He'd been in orbit when the accident occurred, too far away to effect any sort of rescue. The two other crew members on that mission refused to leave their injured comrade behind. They opted to walk him back, taking turns creating a three-legged creature that moved far too slowly. Their emergency oxygen depleted before they reached base and all three suffocated. Like today, Kemper buried them, too, planting their bodies in the red soil forever.

Those situations were different somehow. The universe was always trying to kill spacefarers. This wasn't the universe, though. This was an enemy. A cunning, murderous enemy.

"Do you think it was ritualistic?" Shu asked him quietly.

Kemper paused to look at her. "The killing, you mean?"

She nodded. "Petry... it was the same as those statues in the ruined city."

He considered, then resumed digging. "Maybe," he admitted.

"Ritual requires belief," said Shu," and purpose. That implies culture."

"I didn't see much culture on display last night." Kemper stabbed the spade into the dirt and scooped it out. "Unless you're saying a wolf pack has culture."

Shu was quiet for a several minutes while he dug. Then, gently, she told him, "That's deep enough.".

Kemper stopped. Together, they lowered Petry into the grave. Before Kemper could reach for the shovel to cover the body, Shu grabbed onto it. She pushed the dirt over the top of the dead engineer with efficient, almost loving, strokes. While she worked, Kemper caught his breath. He noticed Grussmacher had returned, once more standing guard over Worona's unconscious body, pistol in hand.

When it was done, he and Shu stood at the graveside. Kemper knew Petry was an atheist, so he didn't utter any religious platitudes. Instead, he simply said the man's name, his role on the *Doncella*, and added, "His importance cannot be overstated. He will be missed."

After a pause, Shu murmured something in Chinese. Kemper didn't speak the language and only knew a few basic phrases. He didn't recognize her words but he didn't ask what she said. Instead, he glanced toward Grussmacher.

"If you want to say some words," Kemper began, but Grussmacher shook his head.

"He's dead," the pilot said. "Whatever he was, is gone." He made a circular motion with his free hand. "We're alive. We need to figure out what that means."

Kemper's eyes narrowed slightly. "What it means?"

"I checked over the shuttle. The landing strut has structural damage from several deep slashes. Also, one of the coolant tanks was punctured by the creatures. The coolant has all leaked out. That means if we fire up that engine, it'll overheat long before we exit the atmosphere."

"We can break into orbit with one engine," Kemper said, recalling the shuttle's specs and Petry's statement just a couple of days ago.

"We can," Grussmacher agreed blandly. "But that engine shows signs of attack, too, so I don't know if it'll engage or not."

"So, we might be stranded here," Kemper said,

keeping his tone matter-of-fact.

"Perhaps. If the potentially damaged engine is no good, I might be able to swap coolant tanks so we have one functioning engine. I'm not sure. Even if we still had Petry to do the job, it'd take time, which we may not have. That's not the last problem, either." He motioned toward Worona and his jaw flexed. "She's another issue. Right now, she's stable but her wounds are severe. She may live. *Probably* will live, given the opportunity to heal. But I don't think she can survive the g-forces that come with the launch and achieving breakaway thrust."

Kemper glanced at the wounded doctor, then back to Grussmacher. "All right, we'll take off and find somewhere more defensible while she heals. A plateau, or maybe even the ruins from before."

"The landing strut may not handle another landing cycle," Grussmacher said. "If that breaks, we're all stranded. No, this shuttle has one take-off left, and that needs to be the one that gets her back to the *Doncella*."

"You just said Worona won't survive that trip."

"She won't," Grussmacher confirmed.

"We can't move our position and we can't take her with us. So, what are you saying? You want to leave her here?"

"Right now, all I'm saying is she needs to remain planet side until she recovers enough that her body can withstand the trip back to orbit."

"Good," Kemper said, his tone clipped. "Because I won't abandon her. We leave no one behind."

"You may want to rethink that, sir. We're explorers, not Marines."

"I *won't* leave her behind," Kemper repeated forcefully.

"She... can't... *fly.*" Grussmacher's tone was equally adamant.

"Then we are staying here until she recovers." He paused. "Or dies."

Kemper glanced down at Worona. Her slack mouth hung open but he could see her chest rise and fall with each breath.

"Besides," he said, "You're not a doctor. You could be wrong."

"We've all been cross-trained on basic medical," Grussmacher reminded him. "Besides, you know the impact of high g-force. I don't think she's bleeding internally, but I'm not sure. If she has even the slightest nick, the pressure of achieving breakaway speed will split it open."

Shu glanced downward at Worona. "We can shelter in the ship until she heals," she suggested. "It's tight quarters, but it'll keep us safe."

Kemper nodded. It wasn't ideal but it was a viable option.

"No," Grussmacher said quietly.

Kemper gave him a sharp look. "I'm not leaving her behind, goddamnit."

Grussmacher shook his head. "Not her. Us."

Kemper stared at him. His mind flashed back to Grussmacher's earlier exhortation for them to take off in the Doncellita without burying Petry. The pilot had said *you* instead of *we.* In the heat of the moment, the significance of that had slipped past Kemper. "Explain," he directed Grussmacher, dreading the man's words.

"The mission must succeed, Captain."

"The crew's survival is part of the mission."

"It is," Grussmacher agreed. "But not the entirety of it." He glanced over at Shu, then returned his gaze to Kemper. "The Kyran civilization is gone, sir. Probably for centuries. There is no longer any diplomacy possible."

"You're out of your lane, Co-Pilot. Mission parameters are my purview."

"I'm not giving orders," said Grussmacher. "I'm pointing out facts. This isn't about first contact and establishing some kind of diplomatic relations. Kyra 2-B is now a planet for potential colonization. That message needs to get back to Earth. It solves our biggest problem—too many people. There's room here for billions."

"The message will be relayed," said Kemper. "Hell, for all we know, they've already sent colony ships. Who knows how much technology has improved? They may have figured out the planet is habitable only a few decades after we left."

"There was nothing about that in the messages we received," Grussmacher said quietly.

"Even that aside," said Kemper, "Achebe can send the message. We'll wait here until Worona is healed and—"

"Those creatures will attack again tonight," said Grussmacher. "And they'll be bolder than before. Maybe even develop better tactics."

"Tactics?" Kemper frowned. "Their behavior seemed more animalistic to me. Predatory instincts on display, true, but—"

"This was a coordinated attack," Grussmacher interrupted. "It wasn't random. They hit us at the village and Petry here at the *Doncellita*. That shows a higher level of intelligence than some alien wolf pack."

Kemper considered, hearing an echo of his own comment to Shu earlier. He realized Grussmacher's assessment was correct. "We'll shelter in the ship tonight," he said.

"You felt the strength of these creatures, sir. One of them managed to make the entire craft move."

"We don't know that was a Kyran. Or just one."

Grussmacher looked dubious. "The slash marks say it was Kyran."

"We'll be safe in the ship," Kemper insisted.

"Maybe. But what if they puncture the other coolant tank? That alone would damage the ship so badly none of us get off this planet. Do you really want to have to order Achebe to fly the *Doncella* home all by himself?"

Kemper stared at Grussmacher. Despite his own protests, he knew the co-pilot's logic was sound. The only question remaining was whether or not he was willing to accept its cost. "You said *us* before."

Grussmacher nodded. "I'll stay with her."

"No."

"It's the only answer, Captain."

"No. Those things will kill you."

"They might. I'll take her back to the village. We'll hole up in one of those huts. Light a fire near the entrance. That should keep them away. If it doesn't, the doorway creates a choke point. Even alone, I can hold them off with my pistol. Once Worona recovers, we can watch each other's backs."

Kemper watched Grussmacher while he spoke. The co-pilot's expression was one of grave resolve.

"If we leave you here, it's for life," Kemper said quietly. "By the time we return to Earth and mount another expedition or prepare colonization...?"

Grussmacher shrugged. "I know you think I'm a cowboy but you also know I'm right. The mission comes first. This is the best chance for it to succeed."

Kemper knew he was probably correct. Instead of arguing that point any further, he said, "If anyone is staying behind, it's me."

"You're the captain."

"That's why."

"Spare me the heroics, sir." Grussmacher shook his head. "No. I know you're brave. We all are—it's a base requirement. But your role is to lead the expedition home. You're the last person who should stay behind."

"I'm the—"

"It should be me," Shu said, in a small voice. "I'm the least important crew member."

Kemper turned to her. "You made contact with an alien species. You communicated with one of its people. That was the entire point of our mission. Shu, you're the *most* important person on this expedition."

"Sir—" she began, but Grussmacher interrupted her.

"He's right, Ouyang. You're crucial. So is the captain. *I'm* the most expendable. My primary role still has its redundancy in place." He pointed upward. "Achebe."

"He'll still be there once Worona heals," Kemper said, trying to make the line of thinking work, even though he was losing faith in it himself.

Grussmacher gave him a determined shake of his head. "The shuttle is functional *today*. If the engine fires up, you and Shu need to leave *today*. Start for home. If you don't and the *Doncellita* gets damaged by those things... we're permanently stranded." He stared into Kemper's eyes. "Three hundred light years is a long journey. We can't leave Achebe to travel it alone, to bear that responsibility all by himself. And what if his cryostasis chamber fails?"

"We'd be leaving you alone."

"I have Worona."

"If she survives."

"She's a tough one," said Grussmacher. "She'll make it, I think. If she does, then we'll make a life here." He grinned humorlessly. "A real Adam and Eve story."

Kemper stood in silent contemplation. *Everything* on *every* mission was a risk. His role was to take the smartest risks and mitigate the odds. Command sometimes came down to a modified version of the infamous trolley problem. Only in this case, he knew all of the people tied to the tracks. He was responsible for them.

He ran through the scenarios. Grussmacher's proposed plan resulted in the sure loss of two crew members. One of those he might lose to her injuries, regardless of his decision. On the other hand, remaining planet side while waiting until Worona healed, risked all four of them. Even if he made the choice to stay, Worona may still die of her wounds. Further attacks could result in additional injuries or irreparable damage to the ship. That risked the three of them being stranded at best, or dying as well in a subsequent attack. That outcome left Achebe to solo pilot the *Doncella* back to Earth.

He didn't like either of his choices.

"The sooner you decide, the sooner I can start setting up my defenses," Grussmacher said.

Kemper stared into Grussmacher's hard eyes. Then he dropped his own eyes to the prone Worona, before glancing over at Shu. He held her gaze, silently asking her opinion.

Slowly, almost imperceptibly, Shu nodded.

"All right," Kemper said reluctantly. "We'll run a diagnostic on the ship. If she can fly, we'll salvage whatever we can for you before we go."

The *Doncellita* sputtered to life.

While Shu stood guard over Worona, Grussmacher ran another systems check. It took the co-pilot less than twenty minutes to pronounce the shuttle flightworthy.

"Barely," he qualified. "It's running rough. She's going to buck a bit as you're trying to achieve escape velocity. With two engines, the thrust power was well beyond the minimum. With just one engine, you're still above that threshold but only barely so. Keep her steady and hold course."

"Got it," Kemper said.

Together, he and Grussmacher scavenged everything useful from the shuttle. Food, medical supplies, tools, and equipment. Kemper hoisted Worona once more and made the short journey back to the deserted village. Laden with provisions, Shu and Grussmacher followed.

After a short discussion, they chose the sturdiest and best positioned hut. Kemper put Worona inside and helped Grussmacher gather wood for the fire. It was late afternoon by the time they finished.

All their tasks complete, the trio stood awkwardly next to the unlit fire. Kemper had misgivings about his decision but he put those aside. They were committed now. He reached out and clasped Grussmacher's hand.

"Best of luck," he said, in a husky voice.

"Complete the mission," Grussmacher replied, his own words thick with emotion.

Shu dispensed with the handshake and drew Grussmacher into a short embrace. They exchanged no words.

Then Kemper and Shu turned away and started back toward the shuttle. It seemed to Kemper it was the longest walk of his life.

11

"Engines online," Shu reported. "You sure you can fly this thing?"

"I guess we'll find out." Kemper adjusted one of the settings. Then he began a countdown from twenty. When he reached ten, he throttled up to half power. The ship lifted into the air and began to ascend. On one, he pushed the engines to full. The shuttle surged upward. The g-forces tugged at them all through the atmosphere. Kemper hung on, keeping the stick steady, thinking of how these pressures would have killed Worona.

Instead, she was going to die at the claws of some beast, he thought forlornly.

Perhaps. Or perhaps they'd survive. Even thrive. When humans returned to this planet in another millennium, maybe they would find it sprinkled with pockets of humanity.

The ship forced its way into high orbit and the shaking stopped. Without a word, Kemper guided the craft toward the *Doncella.* He radioed Achebe and coordinated the docking procedure without incident.

Then he glanced over at Shu. In a few moments, he was going to have to explain what happened on the surface to Achebe. Then he'd have to describe it again for his official log. Once he returned to Earth, how many more times would he be called upon to relate what occurred on the surface and to account for his decision?

Shu had no words to offer him, only a look of pure understanding.

Achebe took the news stoically. After listening to a brief explanation for the missing crew members, he placed a consoling hand on Kemper's shoulder.

"It was the right choice, Captain," Achebe assured him. "A hard choice, but the right one."

"Time will tell."

Achebe's grin was sad. "It truly will. They have a fighting chance, Captain. That's all any of us can ask."

"Prep the ship," Kemper ordered. "We're going home."

Achebe charted a course out of the Kyran solar system while the trio prepared the *Doncella* for near-light travel. The trio worked efficiently, focusing on the meticulous details to keep from thinking of the larger realities of the mission. Shu spent a significant amount of time recording details of her extended contact with the Kyran in her log.

Kemper's own log entries were succinct. He figured to fully answer for his actions upon their return.

Sporadic messages reached them from the planet's

surface as they sped outward. The transmissions from Grussmacher were brief and incomplete, but Shu was able to decipher the gist of them. The Kyrans did not attack the first night. Worona regained consciousness. Her condition remained stable but serious. Then, two days later, the expected attack finally came. Together, Grussmacher and Worona successfully repelled their assailants.

The news was met by Kemper with considerable relief. Images of his crew members being torn to shreds by the savage, stocky Kyrans had filled his head since lifting off from the planet. That they'd survived even a few days gave him some measure of hope.

The final message arrived the same day Achebe reported all systems prepared for acceleration. The message was broken, but one part that came through was clear.

We have met them.

Kemper knew that could have several meanings. He chose to believe in the most positive—Grussmacher had made meaningful contact with the more peaceful Kyrans of the village. The Elves, as Shu had dubbed them. He expressed as much in his log entry, though professionalism forced him to note his was only one of several possibilities. Perhaps Grussmacher had met the third species, Shu's so-called Dwarves. Or the violent Kyrans had attacked again.

He took the greatest bit of hope from the pronoun Grussmacher used.

We.

That meant Worona was still alive. Her recovery

appeared to be real. This increased the odds of their survival. If they'd made contact with the peaceful Kyrans, perhaps it was the beginning of something positive.

He wanted to believe that.

Needed to.

After completing his final log entry before cryo, Kemper gathered Shu and Achebe for a last meal. The remaining crew ate in quiet contemplation. There were no toasts. Kemper's own emotions were mixed. Part of him deemed the mission an utter failure. The weight of losing crew members sat heavily and squarely on his shoulders. Another part of him—the optimist—wondered if the sacrifice of Grussmacher and Worona might have ultimately made the mission a success. There was a small piece of Kemper, one he didn't want to admit to, that was glad he had survived and was going home again. The pure selfishness of that sentiment shamed him and he gave no voice to it. From their silence and solemn expressions, he wondered if Shu and Achebe felt the same.

At one point, Shu whispered, "We should have waited."

Kemper pressed his lips together. "My decision has been made," he said coldly. "Leave the second-guessing to the administrators back home."

Shu looked at him in momentary confusion, then lowered her eyes to her own hands and shook her head. "No, sir. I meant this entire mission. We shouldn't have launched so soon after those initial signals from the Kyrans. We should have waited. Learned more by observing."

"I thought you were in favor of an immediate response."

"I was," Shu admitted. "I was exhilarated at the prospect of first contact." She glanced up at him and back down again. "I was wrong."

Kemper didn't answer. He considered her words while he ate. In the end, she had been far from alone in her urgency. Whether born of fascination or hope, fear of attack or as a desperate solution to overpopulation, enough people felt enough exigency to drive the mission forward. At this point, he didn't see the point lamenting the decision. Much like his difficult choice to leave Worona and Grussmacher behind, it was done. Pining over actions already taken was wasted energy.

"We couldn't know," he said softly.

Shu looked up, her expression inquisitive.

"Humans," Kemper specified. "This journey. We couldn't know what the outcome might be. Waiting for decades or longer might have been an even bigger mistake. A glorious, missed opportunity." He lifted a cup and took a sip before continuing. "We couldn't know," he repeated. "But your intentions were noble. And hindsight is always flawless."

Achebe sat silently in his own seat. Shu considered Kemper's words. Finally she nodded slowly. "I am grateful to have sat across from another being on a distant planet. Yet, it wasn't worth the cost."

"Of course, it wasn't," Kemper agreed. "But what is done is done."

When the meal was finished, Achebe engaged the Ueshiba deflectors. He reported to Kemper they were fully functional.

"Throttle up the Meitner drive," Kemper ordered.

Achebe complied.

The *Doncella* once again accelerated to nearly .87c, having shown no signs of distress from its voyage to the Kyran system. Kemper should have experienced some satisfaction for this, or at least relief. They had avoided some of the many vagaries of space travel. But the loss of Petry, Worona, and Grussmacher tempered any positive feelings he might have had.

Without ceremony, he ordered them all to cryogenic stasis. Achebe went first. The stately pilot lay back without hesitation. He gave them both a nod and closed his eyes. Kemper activated the cryo pod. Once it was fully engaged, he ran a diagnostic. All systems checked out.

He and Shu moved to her pod. Before she settled into it, she leaned forward and kissed him. It was a chaste kiss, almost sisterly, yet riddled with emotion.

"We'll honor their sacrifice, Captain," she whispered.

Kemper swallowed thickly and gave her a nod. "We will."

"See you on the other side," Shu said. Then she climbed into her pod, lay back and closed her eyes. He noticed her jaw remained tight, however.

Kemper's fingers danced across the controls. The pod sealed. Invisible, cryogenic gas filled the interior. Shu's face relaxed. He ran a diagnostic, which came back yellow. The system automatically ran through the corrective process and the monitor turned green only a few moments later.

"Good night," he whispered to Shu, before moving to his own pod.

Activating the commander's pod could be done manually or with voice activation. Kemper chose the latter, directing the system each step of the way. He knew it would automatically run diagnostics and self-correct if necessary. He did some rough calculations in his head and set the alarm to activate to allow him enough time to wake the others so the *Doncella* could decelerate in the outer solar system.

"Sealing," the computerized voice advised him. "Awaiting command to activate cryogenic state."

"Proceed," Kemper said, without hesitation. He remembered thinking the sooner he went to sleep, the sooner he'd awake. Then—

12

The alarm pulled him from the murky darkness.

Baw-baw, baw-baw.

Kemper felt disoriented, unsure where he was. A moment ago, he'd been dreaming of his parents. A summer trip to the beach. His mother in a wide straw hat. His father, uncustomarily unshaven. The smell of salt air. The caw of seagulls.

As the disorientation of the dream faded, the alarm filled his consciousness. The sound was different than the one he'd heard upon awaking in the Kyran system. The cadence was off somehow. As his foggy mind sharpened into alertness, he realized why. There were two separate alarms. The soft tones were offset, creating a two-count rhythm.

Baw-baw, baw-baw.

His first instinct was to rush the reanimation process, but he resisted the urge. Methodically, he took the system through each plodding step, eager for it to be complete. When the slight hiss of rushing air told him the seal was broken, he stabbed at the button to open the pod.

One of the alarms, the one signifying the reanimation of the command pod, suddenly ceased. The second continued.

Baw. Baw. Baw.

Kemper struggled to his feet. Despite the muscular stimulation during cryo, his legs felt stiff and shaky. He held onto the edge of his pod and drew in a deep breath. His gaze drifted to the main navigation station, wondering if it were the source of the trouble. If the Ueshiba deflectors had failed completely, the ship wouldn't be intact. But if they'd encountered a large enough object to necessitate changing their trajectory, or if it was too large to avoid, a course change would be necessary. Protocol required that be done by a human crew member.

He took a few staggering steps to reach the console. There were no flashing lights. His eyes swept over the navigation chart. They were almost perfectly on course and nearly ready to begin the deceleration into the Sol system. The alarm wasn't in regard to their flight status.

Kemper swung around, a black sense of dread forming in his gut. He made his way back to the cryo pods. Achebe's pod showed green across the board.

Shu's was red.

Kemper leaned close, peering through the glass. A skeletal form lay inside. She looked shrunken and deflated. All that remained of her skin resembled shriveled leather drawn taut against her bones. Her skull lay on a bed of wispy black hair.

Kemper drew in a wavering breath and let his hand rest on the pod. He didn't mourn for the knowledge that was lost—Shu's logs contained most of what she'd learned. His grief was for the person who'd held that knowledge, who made something beautiful out of it. She'd been the most important member of the crew, the core of the mission.

He really had failed.

Kemper stood next to Shu's pod for a long while. Then, finally, he punched in the proper codes to re-seal and preserve her remains. He knew she would get a hero's funeral, as would Petry. Grussmacher and Worona would be honored as well for their heroic actions.

It struck him then those last two lost crew members would also require funerals. The pair had now been dead for centuries.

He shook his head slowly.

Interstellar travel was a mind bender. As soon as they decelerated into their home solar system, he and Achebe would be almost fourteen Earth centuries old. Yet, his own memory told him Shu had kissed him goodbye less than an hour ago.

Kemper swallowed and turned away. He reactivated Achebe's cryo pod, monitoring the process until the pilot was fully awake.

Outwardly, Achebe took the news of Shu's death in the same stoic fashion as before, though Kemper could see the sadness etched in his eyes. He paused to murmur a few words in a tongue Kemper didn't know before walking slowly and carefully to the pilot's station.

Kemper abandoned the captain's chair and slid into the navigator's seat.

"Status?" he asked.

Achebe was frowning. "There's been some damage to the hull," he said. "Not enough to warrant an emergency cryo exit, but..."

"Did the Ueshiba deflectors fail?"

"No, sir. I'd say they actually worked as intended. We must have encountered unexpected debris in our flight path. The deflectors minimized what would have otherwise destroyed the ship. But we took some damage in the process."

"How bad?"

"The *Doncella* sealed off the compromised areas, as per safety protocol."

"Which areas?"

"Let's just say, if we'd taken the time to bring back any biological samples, they'd be freeze dried right now." He glanced over at Kemper. "We're in no immediate danger, Captain, but I'm glad we're nearly at journey's end. This ship is no longer space-worthy for the long haul."

"She'll hold together the rest of the way?"

Achebe nodded. "She'll achieve orbit. Whether she breaks apart before her fuel runs out is another matter. But we'll be planet side by then."

"Home, you mean."

Achebe didn't answer.

Kemper gave the order for deceleration and Achebe complied. The *Doncella* slowed without incident and soon they were streaking through the orbital ring of Neptune.

He soon discovered the airwaves were strangely silent. Kemper furrowed his brow in concern. There should be detectable chatter on multiple bands. Not only that, but wouldn't Earth's defensive reach have expanded since their departure? What about colonization? There'd been a few mining and scientific outposts scattered throughout the solar system in Kemper's time. He imagined that trend would have continued as humanity's reach expanded.

In any event, it seemed to him they would hail any vessel entering the solar system.

Then he remembered their own arrival in the Kyran system and the speculation that the Kyran civilization had gone silent to remain incognito. Was it possible Earth had adopted the same Dark Forest philosophy Shu had referenced? He recalled there existed a significant contingent in his own time who had been fierce proponents of this approach. Petry had given voice to it in their discussions. It was entirely possible this way of thinking eventually won out on a planetary level.

They'll still recognize their own ship, he thought. There would be historical records. Even if Earth pulled back from exploration and attempting further contact, their mission to the Kyran system would be known. In short, their return would be expected.

Kemper discussed the troubling silence with Achebe over the days that followed. Ultimately, he waited until the *Doncella* reached the orbit of Jupiter before he decided to hail Earth directly. He opened the primary channel. He spoke slowly, knowing the English he uttered would likely sound archaic to those receiving it. They very well might have artificial intelligence for translation—almost certainly, in fact—but he wanted to make it as easy as possible.

"This is Captain Adrian Kemper of the International Space Ship *Doncella*, on approach to Earth at a distance of five hundred million miles. We are returning from our mission to the Kyran system. Our launch date was approximately one thousand four hundred years ago, Earth time. Please respond."

Kemper settled back in his chair and waited. Based on their relative location, his message would take over forty minutes to reach Earth. Meanwhile, Achebe kept the *Doncella* on course for the home planet.

Two hours later, there was still no reply.

He waited another hour, then repeated his message. No reply.

After that, he set the communication relay to auto-hail.

"Possibilities?" he asked aloud.

"There are three," Achebe answered, even though Kemper's question was largely rhetorical. "They did not receive our transmission. They received the transmission and are unable to respond. They received the transmission and are unwilling to respond."

Kemper nodded at the pure logic of his reply. "I don't know which of those frightens me the most."

"All three are equally chilling," agreed Achebe, his sonorous voice only adding to the pronouncement.

Kemper saw no other viable decision other than to continue. Achebe maintained course and Kemper kept the auto-hail engaged. The program transmitted his recorded message at regular intervals on multiple bandwidths, constantly adjusting for their distance from Earth.

Days passed. The two men lived in relative silence as the ship cruised through the solar system. They slipped past the asteroid belt without incident. As they approached the orbital path of Mars, Kemper ran calculations to detect the planet's current location. He'd hoped to see the red planet, wondering if he might see signs of colonization. Unfortunately, it was positioned three hundred and four days away in its solar revolution, completely opposite the Doncella's flight path.

His disappointment was short-lived, however. Earth itself was in view now, first with the intensity of a morning star and growing brighter each day. When he awoke one morning and hints of blue were visible, the image caused an audible hitch in Kemper's chest.

"She *is* beautiful," rumbled Achebe from the pilot's station.

"And still there." Though many of the self-imposed existential threats of the Great Filter variety had been placed in abeyance by the time Kemper's mission launched, he'd wondered if the human race would somehow regress and fall prey to their own devices. Or develop new ones. But as the *Doncella* drew closer and closer to their home planet, the lustrous blue told him, at the very least, humankind hadn't destroyed the planet.

No one was answering his transmissions though.

"Could they have developed a new form of communication?" he asked Achebe, brainstorming. "Are we sending smoke signals in a digital age?"

"Perhaps," the pilot allowed. "They'd still see the smoke, would they not?"

Kemper couldn't argue that.

When they neared the orbital path of the moon, he ordered Achebe to lower speed. Before them, the daytime Earth was on full display. The color of the planet, the continents and oceans, all looked familiar and virtually unchanged to Kemper. He said as much to Achebe.

"They would be, of course," the pilot said. "The time we've been away is inconsequential in geological terms."

Kemper nodded absently while he stared down at the comforting familiarity of Earth. There were no signs of human civilization visible at this distance, but that had been true when their mission departed, as well.

"One thing bothers me," Achebe said. "The lack of satellites. And there's no space station in orbit."

Kemper glanced down at his sensor scope. Several satellites appeared on the readings and he pointed that out.

"They are there," Achebe agreed, "but not transmitting anything, at least not that I can detect. They are essentially flying garbage."

Kemper considered. Even if human civilization decided to withdraw from exploration or communication beyond the solar system, that didn't negate the need for planet-wide communication. They'd still need satellites.

"Perhaps we're thinking about this wrong," Achebe said. "If technology has progressed exponentially, the need for satellites may well be obsolete."

"Possible," Kemper agreed. He took a deep breath. The automated transmissions were presently reaching the planet surface in less than two seconds. His calibrations to the auto-hail now sent his message every fifteen minutes. There had still been no reply on any band.

"When we cross the terminator into night, we'll be able to see the lights of the population centers," Achebe said. "That will tell us something."

"Good," Kemper said. "Meanwhile, let's re-scan all frequencies. Perhaps we'll find indirect messages."

Two hours later, Kemper happened across a transmission. The language was gibberish to his ear, but clearly human. Another voice responded. The conversation was brisk and then the frequency went quiet.

As the terminator approached, an odd tension seized Kemper. He expected, when the blazing power of the sun was eclipsed, they would see another explosion of light from the surface. The sheer volume of population growth over the centuries would have resulted in the majority of the planet becoming urbanized. The fact that so many humans were living below them and yet would not—or could not—respond to his hails made Kemper feel more alone than he could ever remember.

When the direct rays of the sun were completely blocked by the planet below, Kemper stared down in disbelief.

The planet was nearly dark. Pockets of dotted light

were sprinkled across the land masses, but it was a fraction of what he'd expected. Far less than the pattern he'd seen from orbit in the weeks before the *Doncella* began its outward journey to Kyra-2B.

"Are they masking light?" he asked. "As part of a Dark Forest approach?"

"If so, why not mask all of it?" Achebe responded. "Any passing vessel would see even this much as proof of life."

"Those light centers could be poverty centers," Kemper suggested. "Perhaps they can't afford to mask..." he trailed off, shaking his head at his own flawed reasoning. If a government entity determined masking the existence of their civilization was paramount for safety, it would be a function of government to do so. There would be no leaks, because a single leak was one too many.

"There is another possibility," Achebe said. "The simplest one."

Kemper nodded knowingly. "Depopulation."

"Not necessarily a negative development," the pilot said. "Worona would have been able to offer a more precise, nuanced view, but the concept of resources versus population isn't difficult math. Perhaps humankind instituted a form of population control to exist at a level commensurate with what the planet can support."

"Could be," Kemper repeated. "Perhaps. Maybe. If." He shook his head. "I'm tired of guessing. Let's go find out the answers."

13

Ultimately, they waited another full circumnavigation before they chose Europe. The northern coastline was dotted heavily with lights that wrapped around the western coast of France and across the channel to England. There were other areas of light—China was the thickest—but Europe somehow felt right to Kemper. The mission may have launched from Florida but the headquarters for the CSA was in London.

If England or Florida even exist anymore. Fourteen hundred years is forever in geopolitical terms.

As they prepared to depart the *Doncella,* Kemper transferred the ship logs to the smaller craft. He sensed Achebe looking at him and turned his head. "What is it?"

"There's one last problem," the pilot said.

"It's never one *last* problem," said Kemper. "It's always just one *more.*"

Achebe smiled grimly. "Our landing craft has one good engine and it's damaged, at that."

"It got us into orbit from Kyra," Kemper said.

"Barely."

"It's our only ride down," Kemper told him.

"It may not make it."

"Since it's radio silence from the CSA, or anyone, the alternative is to sit up here in orbit and hope for a rescue before our supplies run out."

"Not an attractive proposition," Achebe admitted.

"This is the only choice," Kemper said. "And I've already made it."

"No argument, sir. I'm just letting you know what we're facing. The engine may not ignite. It may fail under the stress of re-entry."

"We'll cross that river if we come to it."

"Or drown in it," mused Achebe. Then he shrugged and added, "Yes, sir."

Kemper gazed wistfully at the bridge one last time before he gave the order to board the *Doncellita*. Once he and Achebe were strapped into the small vessel, he opened the bay door remotely and used compressed air boosters to gently leave the mother ship, connected only by a single tether.

"Engaging engine," Achebe advised, "at zero thrust."

His use of the singular only highlighted the damage the landing craft had suffered on Kyra-2B. He held his breath while Achebe went through the ignition process.

What an incredible irony it would be, he thought. *To travel three hundred light years and back, only to be stranded in orbit above Earth.*

"Here goes nothing," Achebe said. Then he shrugged, "Actually, here goes everything."

He flipped the final switch.

The single remaining engine sputtered, caught, and

then fired up.

Kemper let out the breath he'd been holding. Relieved, he reached out and punched the button to disconnect the tether. He was answered by a discordant beep.

"I don't like the sound of that," Achebe said.

Kemper jabbed at the button again, getting the same beep in reply. "The tether isn't releasing." He glanced at Achebe. "Alternate means to detach it?"

Achebe was quiet a moment. "We can't do so manually. This vessel isn't set up for hosting a spacewalk. And the suits we're wearing aren't rated for more than brief periods outside pressurized environments." He shook his head. "Captain, we can't get physically to that tether from here."

"What about the robotic drones?"

"Still on the *Doncella.*"

"Can we control them remotely?"

Achebe shook his head. "Only from the bridge."

"Of course."

"This simply isn't a scenario engineers envisioned," said Achebe.

"We could re-dock," Kemper suggested. "Re-pressurize and release the tether by hand."

"We could. That would require shutting down the engine. Our only engine. While it started this time, I'm not supremely confident it will the next. Without Petry to repair it..." He trailed off and shrugged. "Both of us could attempt repairs but I am dubious we'd succeed. And without a way to descend to Earth, it's a long, cold wait to see what we run out of first—oxygen, water, or food."

"What if we re-docked with the engine still engaged?" Kemper knew the answer but felt he had to ask. Perhaps Achebe saw something he didn't.

"Almost immediately, we'd cause damage to the interior of the Doncella, rendering it beyond habitability. There wouldn't be time to get to the spacewalk suits or a secure airlock to change into them." Achebe shook his head. "Re-docking means cutting the engine. Doing that for any reason is a risk."

"Could you accelerate? Snap the tether?"

Achebe nodded. "I can make the attempt," he said. "The tether almost certainly isn't long enough to provide sufficient distance to reach a high enough speed to break free. The only resistance is our relative mass. It's a substantial difference but likely not enough to cause the line to snap."

"There must be another option."

"There is. We tow the *Doncella* into the atmosphere with us." Achebe spoke quietly, as if his suggestion was no great matter.

Kemper knew better.

"She has six times our mass," he said.

"Eight," corrected Achebe. "Also, she's not designed to enter the atmosphere. There are no heat shields or structural support to withstand the process. Re-entry will tear her apart."

"With us attached."

"For a while," Achebe agreed. "It will definitely make a wild ride even wilder. The tether's anchor site will probably come loose at some point. Most likely on the *Doncella* end, but maybe on ours. Either way, that'll cut us free.”

“If it doesn't?”

“Then our full descent is linked. Could be a messy landing.” Achebe shrugged. “Considering the other concerns I have about the engine and our general structural integrity, the landing will be messy either way.”

Kemper considered the pilot's words. “Which option is riskiest, in your opinion?”

“You mean between turning off an engine that may not start again, leaving us stranded in orbit until we die, or hurtling through the atmosphere roped to a fiery ball of metal eight times our mass, hoping to land without breaking apart ourselves?”

“I see your point.”

Achebe arched a brow.

Kemper took a few moments to think. Betting the engine would restart seemed the safer risk, but it was an all-or-nothing scenario. If it failed, they were doomed to die of exposure in orbit, a mere forty-two thousand miles from completing the mission.

“If we had contact with anyone planet side,” Achebe said, “there'd be more options. Seeing that we are on our own...”

“Tow her,” Kemper ordered. “I'd rather risk a fiery death now than a slow, cold one later.”

“Aye, Captain.”

Achebe made three attempts at short burst acceleration, gamely trying to snap the tether. The link was too well manufactured, however, and basic physics was not on their side.

“Thanks for trying,” Kemper murmured.

Achebe began the arduous process of tugging the *Doncella* while calculating re-entry. Kemper remained silent, waiting in case his pilot needed any help.

As usual, he did not.

"Calculations complete," he told Kemper minutes later. "Approaching low orbit." He glanced over. "I could aim for London," said Achebe dryly.

"You're not that good of a pilot."

"I am the greatest pilot to have ever lived," Achebe pronounced grandly, the self-deprecation apparent beneath his proclamation. Under that, Kemper sensed some truth in his words. "I have, after all, traveled over six hundred light years and returned intact."

"Land us first," Kemper said. "Then we'll talk about a statue for you."

"An airport would be more fitting," murmured Achebe, and they began the descent.

Compared to when they landed on Kyra-2B, the turbulence began sooner and was considerably more prevalent.

As the small craft shook and bounced, Kemper struggled to focus his vision—first on monitoring the status lights on the panel in front of them, then craning his neck to look out the small window at the *Doncella*. The larger vessel seemed to be shuddering more than falling. Pieces tore away even as the hull began to glow with heat. Kemper watched until the ship was engulfed in flame, then turned away.

"Temperature within safety parameters," Achebe

reported, his words torn and jagged as the craft was battered by the atmosphere and jerked by the tether that lashed them to the *Doncella.* "Approaching cautionary levels, however."

Kemper closed his eyes briefly and took a steadying breath. Then he opened them and scanned the monitors again.

A flashing red light caught his eye. Before its meaning could register, Achebe's deep voice rang out.

"Engine out. Attempting reignition."

Kemper sat and watched the monitors, waiting.

"Startup failed," Achebe intoned. "Second attempt."

A moment later, there was a sharp plink. The shuttle continued to shake but he could sense it was less violent. He turned to look for the *Doncella.* All he saw was a flaming ball, drifting further away each moment.

"We're clear of her," he reported, his words jostled and uneven.

"Roger that," Achebe said. The pilot stared straight ahead. One hand clutched firmly to the old-style flight yoke, prepared to assume manual control if the engine came back online. With the other, he flipped a switch.

Nothing happened.

"Engine's gone," said Achebe. "Switching to emergency landing protocol."

Kemper knew what that meant.

A crash landing.

They continued to drop, not speaking while Achebe wrestled with the yoke. Then the turbulence suddenly lessened, and almost stopped entirely. Achebe pulled back on the emergency yoke. Kemper felt the *Doncellita* respond sluggishly.

"We're operating on pure aerodynamics now," Achebe said.

Kemper punched a button on the nav computer and read the result. "We're above the Atlantic, approaching mainland Europe."

"I think I can get us above the North Sea. Confirm that heading?"

"Confirmed."

"Aye, sir."

The two men remained silent as Achebe guided the shuttle through the air. After the silence of space, the constant hum of atmosphere brushing by the exterior seemed foreign to Kemper. He glanced out of the window to see the blue-green of the ocean below.

We're home.

He had expected to feel relief, or joy, or even bittersweet nostalgia. Instead, he remained emotionally flat. Only a sense of failure hovered beneath his stoicism.

"Deploying chute," Achebe said.

Kemper braced himself. The sudden lurch jarred him, but he welcomed it. The chute was only intended to slow the craft once it touched down on a runway. Using it during the descent risked tearing it to shreds but also might reduce their velocity enough to make a splash down survivable.

After hurtling downward so fast, the slower drop speed gave Kemper a chance to catch his breath. Another silence settled on them as the *Doncellita* fell toward Earth. Achebe battled the yoke while Kemper tamped down his anxiety that the chute might rip apart at any moment. After several minutes, he checked the scopes and broke the silence. "Still no aircraft approaching," he reported.

"Nice to know we won't be shot out of the sky, at least," Achebe noted dryly.

"True." Kemper ran a quick diagnostic to ensure the scanners were performing properly. When the test returned as all processes functional, he said, "The silence is deafening, though."

Achebe didn't reply.

When the final airborne moments came, the craft seemed to speed up suddenly. Kemper knew it was an optical illusion, but he braced himself anyway.

"Splashdown immin—"

The *Doncellita* struck the water at a slight angle, skipping across the surface twice before coming to a hard stop. The force of the landing rattled Kemper's bones, but he kept his eyes locked on the instrument panel. The fact that he was conscious and still staring at the flashing lights told him all he needed to know—the shuttle hadn't shattered apart.

Then the board suddenly blinked out.

"Power is offline," he told Achebe. The lights from his helmet flickered on, illuminating the dead control panel in front of him.

"Hull is breached," Achebe called back.

"Abandon ship!" Kemper immediately ordered.

He unbuckled the flight restraints and slid out of the navigator's seat. To his left, he caught sight of Achebe doing the same. Kemper scrambled across one of the empty seats and reached underneath another for the emergency life-raft, gripping the handle even as he saw dark ripples shimmering past his feet.

Kemper shed the flight gloves. Dull red lights barely lit the interior of the cabin as he flipped the catch to release the helmet. Air hissed out. He didn't wait for slow decompression but tossed the helmet aside. He worked out of the suit, his fingers dancing across the fasteners. Despite the near silence around him, in the back of his mind, he could hear the *Doncellita's* alert tone.

Baw. Baw. Baw.

He pulled his legs free of the suit and kicked it away. Achebe already stood next to the hatch, watching him. He held another container by its handle. Kemper had the crazy thought they resembled two tourists clutching their luggage, about to go on vacation.

"Pop it," he ordered.

Achebe threw the lever. He didn't have to lift it. The outside pressure forced it open. Water flowed in rapidly, rising to their waists in mere seconds. The ice cold shock set Kemper to shivering violently.

"See you... topside... Captain," Achebe said, his teeth already chattering.

There was no time to reply. Kemper took a deep breath and was engulfed in water.

The dim red lights of the shuttle remained in operation. He hoped they'd last long enough for their escape. Kemper swam toward the hatch. Achebe remained at the opening, holding the cover in place with a foot while he waved Kemper through with his free hand. Kemper wished the pilot had gone through first but there wasn't time to argue. He tucked the life-raft close to his chest and kicked hard, shooting through the hole. A few more kicks and he changed direction, swimming clear of the slowly sinking craft.

Then he waited.

Murky sunlight pierced the surface somewhere above him and filtered down to his location. He didn't look up, keeping his eyes glued to the sinking *Doncellita* and the soft red glow from inside her. His lungs ached for air. He felt panic creeping in on the edges of his thoughts, the instinctual drive for self-preservation.

Wait.

A moment later, a figure streaked out from under the ship. Achebe kicked upward until he neared Kemper. Kemper frantically slapped at his leg, but the water slowed the gesture. He hoped Achebe understood his meaning.

The pilot wrapped both arms around Kemper's legs. The two men sank momentarily before Kemper found the release handle on the life-raft and pulled it. The device self-inflated in less than two seconds. The buoyancy pulled them upward, bursting above the surface seconds later.

Kemper drew in a ragged breath, holding onto the edge of the life-raft. A moment later, Achebe's head broke water beside him. The pilot's hand shot out and grabbed onto a grip on the rubber craft. He glanced over at Kemper.

"Welcome home," he croaked.

14

Once they'd clambered onto the life-raft, Kemper saw the container Achebe had wisely salvaged.

A survival kit.

Achebe opened the container and they inspected its contents. Food, water, micro-thin blankets that resembled foil, and a flare gun.

"How many flares?" Kemper asked, wrapping himself into one of the blankets.

"Three," Achebe said. The pilot's teeth chattered as he spoke.

Kemper handed him one of the blankets and waited until Achebe had opened it and pulled it around his shoulders.

"Launch a flare now," he ordered. "Someone may have seen our descent. Let's show them where we landed."

Achebe loaded the flare gun, lifted it into the air, and fired. The white ball rose swiftly into the sky like a comet, leaving a smoke trail, then burst into a blazing brightness at its apex. The signal seemed to hang in the air, drifting downward slowly until it finally fizzled out just a few yards above the ocean.

"We'll wait an hour and fire the second," Kemper said.

The two men huddled atop the life-raft, blankets drawn tightly around them. After a while, Kemper's shivering subsided, but the cold remained. He guessed they had another four hours of daylight left before the sun dipped over the horizon. Based on the weather, he guessed the season to be early autumn. That meant the temperature might drop significantly overnight.

He wondered if freezing to death on the ocean was more tragic than a slow death in orbit.

That's defeatist thinking, he chided himself.

Stop it.

After what he guessed was an hour, Kemper took the flare gun himself and fired the second shot. He and Achebe watched it hopefully as it arced into the sky. This time, it seemed to fall much more quickly and was extinguished far too soon.

"We'll save the third for after nightfall," Kemper said. "Or if we spot an approaching ship."

Achebe nodded his understanding.

As the sun set, the two ate a small dinner from their limited rations and sipped fresh water from their meager supply. Achebe found a desalinization device within the survival kit, which alleviated one of Kemper's biggest fears; at least they wouldn't die of thirst. His other concern, the temperature, loomed ahead of them.

Kemper scanned the horizon in one direction while Achebe watched the other. Nothing but water was visible to Kemper's eye.

When darkness fell, Kemper told Achebe, "I'll take first watch. You get some sleep."

"I'm almost afraid to sleep, sir. If it gets cold..."

Kemper understood. The foil blankets reflected their body heat back onto them, retaining well over ninety percent of it. But it wasn't one hundred percent, and there were plenty of gaps. Depending on how cold it got...

"We'll keep each other awake," Kemper agreed.

They took turns telling stories. Achebe shared about his childhood, growing up in West Africa. The mix of tradition and innovation he described fascinated Kemper.

"Will you go back?" he asked.

"Oh, almost certainly. That is where my family is."

"Family?" Kemper was struck by the oddity of the sentiment. One of the criteria for crew members was a distinct lack of family connections. The psychological impact of losing everyone close was deemed a risk that might endanger the mission. Even someone without significant attachments might be affected, as evidenced by his own weeping outburst when he initially came out of cryo in the Kyran solar system.

Another factor seemed more impactful than that.

"You've been gone fourteen hundred years, Achebe. I'm sorry, but your family is gone."

"No, my friend. Family is forever." When Kemper didn't reply, Achebe added, "I was an only child. That is how I was able to join the mission. But I had many cousins. If anything, my family is much bigger now than when I left. The value of family was part of my culture for hundreds of years before I was born. Thousands, perhaps. It will not have changed in the years since."

Kemper hoped not. He wished that for Achebe.

He wished that for himself, too, but knew it wasn't possible. At least for Achebe, it might be.

"What about you?" the pilot asked him.

Kemper thought about it. For so long, his only focus had been on the mission and the crew. Now, his mind drifted back to when Vasim Gupta from CSA had recruited him, and his one stipulation.

"I have a house," he said.

"Ah. Does it still stand, do you think?"

Kemper lifted one shoulder in a barely perceptible shrug. "It was already old when we left. But it was built mostly with stone, so... yes, I think it may still be there." He drew the blankets tighter around him. "The CSA helped me put it into a trust so it would still be mine when we returned."

Achebe gave a low whistle. "The rest of us were only allowed to place money into our trusts."

"I chose the house instead," said Kemper. "So, now you are a rich man but I have some place to live."

Achebe's low chuckle reverberated in the darkness. "Perhaps money does not even exist anymore. Perhaps we have grown past such requirements as a people."

"Money has been in existence since the Mesopotamian shekel. I'm sure it's still around today."

"You are probably correct. But a man can hope."

"It's a strange man who hopes to be poor."

"Poor in that way would mean our land is rich in spirit," said Achebe. "That our species has become something grander than we were."

Kemper liked that sentiment.

"Tell me about your house, Captain."

Kemper glanced up at the stars, reveling in their familiarity. He told Achebe about the stone structure and the way the light filled the main room. He described how the home put him at peace somehow.

Achebe laughed lightly. "I would have thought you were most at peace while hurtling through the stars, responsible for a crew and a mission."

"You're mistaking peace for purpose," Kemper said.

That made Achebe laugh louder. "So I am," he rumbled. "So I am."

Kemper was quiet for a while, pondering a decision. Then he asked, "Fire the final flare now or save it for a ship sighting?"

Achebe didn't answer right away, contemplating the question. Kemper waited, listening to the slosh of water against the rubber life-raft as they swayed atop the waves. Finally, the pilot said, "If it were my decision, I would use it now. If anyone saw our descent or our first two flares and is searching for us, this would help."

"If not?"

Achebe shrugged, his shadowy figure shifting with the motion. "Then not. It is a decision that has no right or wrong answer, only a question of luck."

"Luck," Kemper murmured. "We could use some of that."

"We could," agreed Achebe. "Though I would say we have experienced much thus far. Less luck would have meant more tragedy."

Kemper considered, then reached for the flare gun. He loaded the final flare and pointed the device into the air. He squeezed the trigger. First came a pop, then a sizzling sound as the flare ignited on its way up.

He stared at the rising orb, brighter than any star as it reached its apex and hung in the air. His thoughts ran to the life-cycle of a star, and how one day the Earth's own sun would extinguish, much like the flare eventually did as it drifted downward toward the black water of the surrounding ocean.

After that, the two of them struggled to remain awake. Kemper eventually slipped into a half-awake haze. Floating in the small life-raft, tossed lightly by the water, he felt strangely as if he'd returned to space. A sliver of moon shone down, failing to pierce much of the surrounding darkness that pressed in on him. Only the stars in the sky above gave him any sense of perspective as he tried to keep his thoughts positive.

He dozed but did not dream.

No ship came that night.

He did not remember waking.

In all likelihood, he woke minutes before and stared at the light starting to creep over the horizon. There wasn't enough of it to change the black hue of the water, but now, instead of darkness, his world had distinct shadows.

Before the sun broke, a sharp horn blasted. Both men started at the noise. Kemper swung his gaze frantically in a full circle. A moment later, he saw the source of the sound.

A gunmetal gray boat sailed directly toward them.

Kemper rose to his knees and waved his hands above his head to signal them. Next to him, Achebe did the same.

The vessel's horn sounded again.

Kemper kept waving his hands. He thought an early morning mist was coming off the water, splashing his face.

Then he realized he was weeping.

The boat looked to be an ancient fishing trawler. Its hull was riddled with rust discolorations. Netting hung from booms. Several crew members in battered yellow slickers stood at the railing, watching them.

When the boat drew near enough, a crewman threw out a line. Both Achebe and Kemper grabbed onto it. Kemper held it while the pilot looped it into one of the life-raft's handles. The crewman worked a crank to pull the life-raft closer. Kemper and Achebe kept a grip on the rope, not trusting the strength of the handle to withstand the tow.

Once they reached the side of the boat, someone dropped a rope ladder. Kemper motioned for Achebe to go first, but the pilot refused.

"You are the captain," he said. "It is your place to be the first face they see upon our return."

Our less than glorious return, Kemper thought, but he remained silent.

Climbing the rope was a more difficult task than it

should have been. The rocking of the sea, his deteriorated strength, and his stiffness all conspired against him. With great effort, he took one rung at a time. When his shoulders broke above the railing, rough hands grabbed onto him and pulled him over.

"Thank you," Kemper wheezed.

A few moments later, Achebe emerged over the side. Kemper heard a few dark mutters as he appeared. He glanced around for the source but was unsuccessful. All he saw were hard faces and suspicious eyes.

"Hvem bist duch?" one man asked. He wore a gray cap with a bill. A battered black metal insignia of an anchor adorned the front.

"Are you the captain?" Kemper asked.

The man glanced around at his crew. *"Jemund der forstår?"*

The others all shook their heads.

The leader turned his attention back to Kemper, pointedly ignoring Achebe. *"Hvem bist duch?"* he asked again.

Kemper guessed at the nature of the question. It was the one he would ask in the same situation.

"I'm Captain Adrian Kemper of the spaceship *Doncella*," he said, touching his own chest. "Kemper," he repeated slowly.

The fisherman glanced down at Kemper's hand and back to his face.

Kemper motioned to Achebe. "This is Pilot Lethabo Achebe."

The man didn't follow Kemper's gesture but kept his gaze fixed on him.

"We're explorers," Kemper explained. "returning from our mission in space."

The man's eyes narrowed. "Mission?" he asked, pronouncing it *miss-ee-OHN.*

"Yes," Kemper said, nodding enthusiastically. "Mission," he repeated, mimicking the same pronunciation.

The surrounding men shuffled their feet and murmured.

Kemper kept his eyes fixed on the leader.

The leader touched his chest. *"Kapitajn."*

Kemper nodded, making out the word easily enough. It was as he thought. The man was the vessel's captain.

Kapitajn pointed at Kemper. *"Bist duch Russisk?"*

Kemper squinted. "Russian?" he asked. He shook his head. "No."

Kapitajn's eyes cut to Achebe. *"Ond er? Ist dein tjener?"*

Kemper turned over his hands. "I don't understand."

Kapitajn frowned.

"We are astronauts," Kemper said. "Can you take us to London?"

"Astronauten?" The corners of Kapitajn's mouth turned up in a smile. *"Seriøst?"*

"Yes." Kemper bobbed his head twice and repeated the word. *"Astronauten."*

Kapitajn burst out in laughter. The crew joined in. Kemper glanced around, smiling. He knew he must have made a mistake in guessing the translation and committed some kind of gaffe. He wished suddenly for Shu. She could have deduced enough about this language to make their identities and their needs clear.

A moment later, an image of her desiccated body inside the failed cryo chamber flashed in his mind. A stab of sadness struck him and he clenched his jaw.

Eventually, the laughter tapered off. Kapitajn clapped Kemper on the shoulder. *"Ooh-kah, Astronauten. Londonich, ja?"*

"Yes," said Kemper somberly, grateful at least this much of his message got through. "London."

Kapitajn gave some brusque orders. A crewman herded Kemper and Achebe to the prow. Another crewman recovered their meager belongings from the life-raft. He asked Kemper a question repeatedly. Eventually, through hand signals and tone of voice, Kemper realized he wanted to know if they should recover the raft.

Kemper shook his head.

The crew member returned to the rail and cut the raft loose. Kemper was glad he couldn't see it float away from his vantage point.

They remained in position for the remainder of the day.

All around them, the crew worked. Kemper watched in fascination as they manipulated the boom to lower and retrieve the netting. He noted several crew members also had heavy duty fishing lines in the water. The catch seemed bountiful to him, but, of course, he had no frame of reference.

The wind was brisk, but their blankets kept them reasonably warm. They made a cold breakfast with the remainder of their emergency rations. Around mid-day, a crewman approached and thrust a pair of cups toward them containing a thick fish stew. Grateful, they ate. The warm meal sustained them throughout the remainder of the day.

"Fourteen hundred years," Kemper murmured, as he watched the men work, "and yet we still fish in the same way."

"It was like this for millennia, was it not?"

"I don't know. Perhaps."

Achebe glanced around, then shrugged. "My reaction is to be grateful there are still fish in the sea, Captain. There were dire predictions in our time regarding this."

"Too many people," Kemper mused, remembering.

In late afternoon, the crew raised the nets a final time, and set a steady course south. Their work didn't cease, however. The men bustled around the boat, some checking and securing lines, others completing the gutting of the larger fish. Eventually, all of them turned to the task of cleaning the vessel. Throughout their labors, they studiously ignored the two interlopers.

By the time land came into view, most of the work aboard the vessel was finished. It grew quiet behind Kemper and Achebe as they watched the harbor draw nearer and nearer. When the vessel docked, Kapitajn came to them, flanked by two of his largest crewmen.

"Kommst duch med mig," he ordered. To emphasize his directive, he waved his hand, beckoning

them.

Kemper didn't argue. There was little choice. They may have been rescued or they might now be prisoners. Perhaps both. The only way that remained to them in this mission was forward.

He followed Kapitajn, and Achebe came with him.

The five men left the fishing trawler behind and strode along the wooden docks. Kemper looked around at the wharf. The docks were made of heavy wood worn smooth. The surrounding buildings had a likewise weathered appearance. He guessed they were in an older town, one not benefitting as much from the advances or commerce of the larger cities.

The writing on signage looked vaguely Germanic, though he could only pick out a word or two that was recognizable. Perhaps Danish? He couldn't be certain, and wished again for Shu's skillset, not to mention her quiet, earnest enthusiasm for these experiences.

As the group walked purposefully through the town, a few people called out greetings to Kapitajn. He responded in kind. Other exchanges were clearly questions which he ignored. Curious eyes followed them. Kemper tried smiling at the first few but was met with flat or suspicious stares in return. More than a few cast hostile glares in Achebe's direction.

That made Kemper nervous.

By the time they reached their destination, Kemper realized something else. The demographic makeup of the small town was extremely homogenous. The general features, including skin pigmentation and hair color, existed within a surprisingly narrow band. He wondered how far off the beaten path they had landed.

Kapitajn stopped at an official-looking building Kemper quickly determined was some sort of a constable's station. A heavyset man with dour eyes emerged, wearing a rumpled uniform and a badge. He greeted Kapitajn unenthusiastically. As the latter spoke, the constable unabashedly examined Kemper and then Achebe. When Kapitajn finished, he and the constable had a discussion that devolved into an argument. None of the words made any sense to Kemper but the subject was easy enough to discern—it was either what to do with them or who was responsible for them.

Eventually, Kapitajn threw up his hands, turned, and walked away. Kemper moved to follow him, but Kapitajn gestured for him to stay.

"Duch bliven. Det ist farvel."

Kapitajn strode away without looking back.

The constable sighed. *"Duch bist Kemper?"* he asked.

Kemper nodded, tapping his chest. "Kemper." He motioned to Achebe and spoke the pilot's name.

The constable didn't acknowledge Achebe. He touched his badge and said, *"Jeg bin konstablen Lærke."*

"Lærke?" Kemper asked, guessing at his given name.

Lærke tapped the badge with greater insistence. *"Konstablen,"* he corrected.

"Ah," Kemper said, nodding. "A formal man, then."

Lærke squinted at his words, then dropped his hands. *"Skal duch nach Londonich?"*

"Yes," said Kemper. "London."

Lærke smirked. He waved them inside. The constable's station was small. A desk sat in the outer area. A closed door led to another room Kemper guessed was equally tiny. Lærke led them past that to a barred cell. He used an oversized key to work the lock and swung the door open. Then he motioned them inside.

Kemper hesitated. "I don't want to go in there."

Lærke repeated the gesture, already impatient.

Kemper remained in place, saying nothing.

Lærke sighed. He swung the door open as wide as it went, until he was able to latch it to the cell bars. Then he held up the key, wiggled it, and hung it on a nearby hook. He spread his hands.

Kemper reluctantly went into the jail cell. Achebe followed. Lærke made no move to close the door behind them. He did, however, point emphatically and then show them the palm of his hand in a stop gesture.

Kemper nodded his understanding. "Stay here," he said, pointing to the ground. He sat on the edge of one of the two small cots in the cell. "Got it."

Lærke frowned and left the station.

"Not the hero's welcome we imagined," Achebe said dryly.

Kemper smiled, in spite of everything. The pilot had remained largely silent throughout the day. Now, his baritone voice and dry wit were welcome.

"Where do you think we are?"

Achebe shrugged. "Northern coast of Germany or Denmark," he guessed. "If either country still exists as we knew it."

"That was my thought, as well. One piece I can't

quite figure out is the attitude."

"You mean the hostility? Especially toward me?"

"Yes. Yet, they are helping us. The fishermen rescued us and brought us here. Constable Lærke made it clear we weren't in custody. The behavior and the attitude don't entirely match."

"It is dissonant," agreed Achebe. "Very clannish, no? Distrust of outsiders is prominent, yet the good side of human nature is to help another in need."

Kemper nodded slowly, thinking. He was still mulling it over when Lærke returned, carrying a box. He unloaded three dinners, handing two of them directly to Kemper. Kemper gave one to Achebe.

"Spisen," he said, motioning for them to eat.

Lærke took a seat at his desk and tore into the food with enthusiasm. Kemper and Achebe did likewise. The dish was a goulash of sorts, with fish, beef, potatoes, onions, and a few other vegetables. After subsisting for so long on CSA rations, this food lit up Kemper's tastebuds. When Lærke glanced over at them, Kemper lifted his spoon and smiled. "Delicious," he said. "Thank you."

Lærke seemed to take his meaning and grunted. Then he turned back to his own food.

After dinner, Lærke appeared to be laboring over some form of paperwork. He lifted a telephone that reminded Kemper of the ancient landline devices that predated wireless communication. Lærke was on and off the phone for a long while, engaging in several different conversations.

Kemper remained quiet, thinking through their situation. Achebe was silent as well, eventually lying back on his cot to sleep.

It was well after dark when Lærke finished his conversations. He approached the cell again. Kemper fully expected the constable to swing the door shut and lock them in. However, Lærke merely repeated his emphatic hand signals for them to remain.

Kemper nodded, signaling he understood and would comply. He placed his hands together and tilted his head to simulate lying on a pillow, then made snoring sounds.

Lærke nodded his approval. The constable went to a door near his desk and pulled it open. He flicked on a light and gave his hand a flourish to present the room. Kemper saw it contained an old-style toilet and wash basin.

The bathroom.

Not the outhouse Petry was so disdainful of, but close.

He nodded to Lærke he understood.

The constable snapped off the light and left the door ajar. Then he strode to the front door of the station and locked it. After that, he disappeared out of view to the side of the cell. Kemper heard another interior door open and close. Kemper surmised Lærke lived in accommodations on site. Thudding steps climbing stairs confirmed his guess.

Kemper lay back in the dim light, staring out through the bars. Nearby, Achebe's even breaths told him the pilot was asleep. Kemper wondered for a little while what the morrow would bring, then surrendered to sleep himself.

15

In the morning, Lærke handed Kemper two dense pastries and two cups of a dark, hot tea. He still barely acknowledged Achebe. Kemper gave the pilot his breakfast. Meanwhile, Lærke ate quickly and urged them to do the same.

Once they'd finished, he hustled them out the front door and through the streets. In a nearly identical replay of yesterday's trip from the harbor, some citizens called out greetings to Lærke. A few seemed to ask him the same question over and over again, to which he gave a short, brusque response. The stares, both curious and hostile, followed them through the streets.

Kemper didn't bother smiling back this time.

Their destination became clear long before they reached it. Lærke was taking them to a train station. When they reached the platform, he spoke to an official, explaining and motioning toward Kemper and Achebe. The train man listened without expression. Finally, he gave a curt nod to Lærke's final question and Lærke turned away. He lifted a hand as he passed by his charges on his way back the direction they'd come.

"Farvel," he said, his tone neutral.

The train man was older than either Kemper or Achebe. His white hair was cropped closely and covered with a blue hat that was, in a way, very similar to Kapitajn's. Only the symbol was different, as his resembled a spoked wheel.

He directed them to a bench, where they waited. Then he disappeared into a small nearby office. An hour passed. Then, in the distance, a train approached. Kemper watched it as it came closer and closer to the station. The plumes of smoke fascinated him.

"Coal, do you think?"

Achebe nodded. "Certainly not electric. Nor nuclear."

"Have these people rejected technology?" he wondered. "A religious order, perhaps?"

"I don't think so, sir."

"What do you think, then?"

Achebe met his gaze. "I am quite uncertain. Perhaps we will get our answers in London."

The train came to a sighing stop next to the platform. The old train man emerged from his tiny office and passed them off to a conductor who looked similar enough to have been a brother, or a cousin, at least. The conductor eyed them curiously then waved them aboard. He escorted them to a passenger car and indicated where they should sit.

Kemper and Achebe sat.

Fifteen minutes later, the train lurched forward and

began its southerly trek.

Kemper stared out the window at the passing terrain. After so long being in absolute control over every aspect of his life, the passivity of the last two days felt strange to him. There were actions he could take, he knew, but none of them made greater sense in the moment than letting events play out. Still, being carried by the current was unfamiliar to him—he'd always set his own course.

The countryside that flitted past was sparsely settled. A few houses. Some power lines. Roads ran parallel to the tracks and away from them. Many were paved but a surprising number were gravel or dirt. Kemper saw farm animals and fields of crops, but none looked to be commercial-sized operations.

The train chugged south, stopping at small settlements much like the one from which their journey began. Kemper tried to read the placards identifying each station but none seemed familiar to him. At each stop, people boarded and exited the train. Other passengers looked at the two of them in the same way the people had on the village streets earlier. They chose seats as far from them as possible, giving Kemper and Achebe a wide berth.

Around mid-day, his theory of a small pocket of people who purposefully lived anachronistic lives deteriorated. Everything they saw was at roughly the same technological level. No, Kemper decided, something else was the answer.

The conductor returned a short time later. He handed Kemper two bags for lunch. They ate in silence. Afterward, Achebe deduced where the restrooms were.

Other than this essential deviation, the astronauts remained in their seats. Kemper switched places with Achebe after lunch so the pilot could better enjoy the view of the countryside. It also made it easier when the conductor eventually returned late in the day with another two bags of food, since he, once again, studiously ignored Achebe.

The train eventually reached a more populated city. From the train window, the urban sprawl appeared darker and dirtier than the rural areas they'd passed through. A much larger contingent of passengers left at this stop and even more boarded in their place. The stares and occasional murmurs ran their course again. Out of necessity, reluctant passengers filled up the seats closer to Kemper and Achebe.

The journey continued. Intermittently, the conductor checked on the two of them. He tried to give them some indication of how long they would be there, tapping the analog watch at his wrist and spinning his finger. Kemper thought he understood. Given their speed and where he and Achebe had estimated was their starting point, the trip to London would take at least a full day, likely more.

Night fell and with it any meaningful view outside the window. The interior lights dimmed. The train rumbled on the tracks.

"It's strange," Achebe mused.

"What? To be home again?"

"That, as well," the pilot agreed. "But I was thinking of the technology we've encountered thus far. It is industrialized, but compared to our time—"

"When we left, you mean?"

"Yes."

"Fourteen hundred years ago?" Kemper asked pointedly.

"That's what's so strange, sir. We were concerned with our return resembling something along the lines of a Neanderthal in a dugout canoe, but instead..."

"Instead, it's like we went backward in time five hundred years instead of forward fourteen hundred."

"Exactly."

"Maybe the physicists were all wrong about near-light speed travel, after all."

Achebe let out a wry chuckle. "I wish it were that easy. Instead, I am reminded of what we found on Kyra-2B once we arrived. A devolution of civilization. It's not as pronounced here as it was there, but—"

"Duch." The nearby voice spoke in a snarl. Kemper looked up to see a burly man standing in the aisle, glaring at Achebe. He pointed a finger at the pilot. *"Neigra."*

Kemper glanced at Achebe, whose expression remained stoic. Then he slid from his seat and held up his hands, placating. "Easy," he said, keeping his voice even and non-threatening. "We don't want any trouble."

The burly man jabbed a finger in the air. *"Neigra!"* he repeated, more animated. *"Mineh brodor kæmpede mod jer. Und duch dræbte ham!"*

"Easy," Kemper repeated. "I don't know what you're upset about, but—"

The man's eyes snapped to Kemper. A moment later, his fist lashed out.

Without thinking, Kemper tried to block the punch.

He lifted his arms defensively. A lifetime of martial training kicked in. But his diminished condition extended to his reflexes as well and he wasn't able to block it fully. The man's fist, headed for Kemper's chin, deflected off a forearm and caught Kemper in the forehead instead.

A flash of white passed in front of him. He staggered backward in a pair of half-steps. When his senses returned, he saw a knife had appeared in the man's hand.

"Fir mineh brodor!" the man shouted, and lunged toward Achebe.

The pilot tried to dodge, but his sitting position afforded him little opportunity. He let out a short yelp of pain as the blade struck home.

Kemper charged, tackling the man. The two combatants toppled to the floor. Kemper scrambled to achieve a joint lock on his opponent's knife hand, but the man's thrashing movements made it difficult.

"Furrædur!" bellowed the man.

Kemper didn't bother to try to speak. Already, his breath was coming in ragged gasps. He flailed at the man's wrist, gripping it and attempting to twist. There was no give in the man's forearm, however. It was like trying to bend metal.

Then, suddenly, the man stiffened, a short grunt escaping his lips. His body went slack. Kemper pushed off of him and scrambled away.

The conductor stood over the man, a short cudgel in his hand. He held the weapon poised in the air, ready to deliver another blow. When the man on the ground remained still, the conductor swept his gaze across the passenger car. He barked out a command in a guttural tone. Immediately, the remaining passengers rose and filtered out of the car, using the door nearest them to exit.

Once the last passenger was gone, the conductor lowered his cudgel. He stepped over the prone man and approached Kemper.

"Was sketech der?" he growled.

Kemper held up his hands in the same placating gesture he'd used against their attacker. Then he pointed to the fallen man. "He came after us," he explained.

The conductor glared at him, then cast a sidelong glance at Achebe. He let out an exasperated sigh before sliding his weapon back onto his belt. Then he strode to a metal box attached to the wall and opened it. He returned to Kemper and thrust an assortment of bandages, wrap and tape into his hands.

"Kummere duch en din tjener," he said, his tone dismissive and slightly exasperated.

In the aisle, the man who'd attacked them groaned. The conductor stepped next to him, took him by the arm, and drew him to his feet. He spoke rapidly, berating the man, who offered no argument. Then the conductor ushered him toward the far doorway and out of the passenger car, not looking back.

Kemper turned to Achebe. The pilot was already pulling aside his uniform to inspect the injury to his abdomen. Kemper took the seat beside him, tearing open a bandage.

"Is it deep?"

"I don't believe so," Achebe grunted, holding his hand over the wound. "But it is difficult to say."

Kemper moved the pilot's hand aside. The incision looked surprisingly small, but he knew that could be misleading. If the man's knife had been narrow but long, like those they'd seen wielded on the fishing trawler...

No, he recalled. It was shorter than that.

"You'll be all right," he assured him.

"I appreciate your optimism," said Achebe in return. "But I would be lying if I didn't say the sentiment would be more encouraging if it came from an actual doctor."

Kemper pressed the bandage to the wound, then another. He kept up direct pressure and, when the bandages no longer soaked through, he set about wrapping them in place. Achebe shifted in his seat to assist in the process, his only commentary small grunts of pain.

When he had finished, the two sat in silence for a few moments, gathering themselves. Finally, Kemper said, "What was that all about, do you think?"

Achebe laughed softly. "Oh, I have a pretty good idea, sir. Although, I never thought I'd see such blatant behavior again in my lifetime."

"Racism?" Kemper asked.

Achebe closed his eyes and nodded briefly.

Kemper thought back to the man's demeanor. Perhaps Achebe was right, but to Kemper, the attack had seemed more... personal somehow. He didn't know how to quantify that, other than the nature of the man's emotion, so he didn't bother trying to explain himself.

Suddenly very weary, Kemper wanted to sleep. But he saw Achebe's eyes were still closed, and so he suggested Achebe do so.

"Only me?" the pilot asked, opening his eyes and giving Kemper an inquisitive look. "Are you keeping watch, then?"

"I believe it would be wise," said Kemper. "We could be perfectly safe after the conductor's warnings but I think caution is still our friend."

Achebe didn't argue. Instead, he immediately let his head loll to the side against the seat rest and closed his eyes again.

Kemper fought sleep for the next several hours. The darkness, the rocking motion, and the monotonous drone of the clacking wheels conspired against him. He was reminded of the night they spent on the sea. Was that only two days ago?

Two days, he mused.

Fourteen hundred years.

Time was a mind bender.

When much of the night had passed, Achebe sat up, awake. The pilot blinked and rubbed his eyes. He glanced around, then met Kemper's gaze.

"How are you feeling?" asked Kemper.

"You're concerned about internal bleeding?"

Kemper nodded.

"The pain is dull," Achebe told him, "but it doesn't feel deep." He touched the wounded area gingerly. "No significant tightness to the skin. I don't feel especially weak or feverish. I don't believe there's any internal bleeding, Captain."

"Good. You should go back to sleep."

Achebe shook his head. "I am fully awake now. Let me take the rest of the watch."

"Are you sure?"

"I am. You may sleep, Captain."

Kemper searched Achebe's eyes and saw the resiliency and the truth he expected to see. Satisfied, he leaned his own head back and fell into a dreamless slumber almost immediately.

He woke to the train lurching to a stop.

The cry of gulls replaced the sound of wheels on the track. Kemper rubbed the sleep from his eyes and peered around.

"Where are we?"

"I'm not certain," said Achebe. "But the signs for the last few hours have appeared very French."

"Last few hours?" Kemper glanced out the window, searching for the sun. "What time is it?"

"Mid-morning," Achebe said. He lifted a paper bag from the floor between them. "Our benefactor brought breakfast."

Kemper cocked his head. "Handed it to you, did he?"

"No. He set the bags on your lap."

Kemper frowned. He took the bag and looked inside. He found a dense pastry similar to the ones Lærke had given them.

"For the record, it was actually better than what our constable friend provided."

Kemper bit into it, suddenly ravenous. Achebe was right; the pastry was no less dense but had a softer, more buttery texture to it.

Around mouthfuls of food, he asked, "No sign of any other attackers?"

"Other than the conductor, no one so much as entered the car," said Achebe.

Kemper dipped his chin toward Achebe's bandaged middle. "How's that feeling?"

"Stiff," Achebe admitted, "and painful. Neither sensation is beyond management." He took a shallow breath and let it out. "All in all, I would say I got lucky. If an internal organ had been pierced, I am dubious of the medical capabilities aboard this train. Or outside it, for that matter."

Kemper glanced out the window. From other cars, passengers bustled off the train. The conductor appeared moments later. He gestured for them to follow. Kemper fell in behind him, along with Achebe. The pilot's steps were more measured than usual and Kemper slowed his own pace accordingly. The conductor gave them both an exasperated look, urging them to hurry. Kemper made no move to increase his speed and eventually, the conductor's exhortations ceased. Instead, the man's face settled into a scowl and he led them forward.

The trio left the train platform and passed through a station similar in size to the one from which they'd departed. The conductor led them to another man who stood near the front exit. This man resembled Kapitajn in his attire, though he was nearly as heavyset as Lærke, and his cap was unadorned with any insignia whatsoever. He seemed perplexed by the conductor's instructions, but eventually shrugged and murmured something Kemper couldn't make out. It didn't matter—he doubted he would have understood it. He knew less French than he did German or Danish, and he imagined all three languages had undergone significant changes since they departed Earth.

The Frenchman, if that was indeed what he was, led them from the station whistling tunelessly while he walked. The port town they'd arrived in bustled with activity. It appeared more modern than where they'd first made landfall after being rescued by the fishing trawler. Kemper saw all the signs of urban living: power, lights, antennae, and something he hadn't noticed in the first village—vehicles. A few cars spouting black exhaust passed in the streets as they trudged along a sidewalk. The sidewalk itself reminded Kemper of concrete but was darker, though not so dark as asphalt.

Behind him, Achebe struggled gamely to keep up, but the pilot's steps were labored. Kemper reduced speed even further to ensure they remained together. Their escort noticed this and slowed his own pace accordingly, seemingly unperturbed. His tone deaf, discordant whistling continued, and he appeared completely devoid of any self-consciousness.

Their journey seemed to come full circle when they eventually arrived at their destination – the harbor. This time, however, instead of a fishing trawler, the congenial escort led them to a ferry. A few cars trundled up the ramp but the bulk of the passengers were afoot.

"London?" Kemper asked their guide.

The heavyset man dipped his chin. When he spoke, it sounded to Kemper like he said, *"Woo. Lohn-dray-EEN."*

Kemper thanked him.

"Deh rouen," the man said. He tipped his fingers to his temple with a casual salute, turned and strode away.

The two astronauts boarded the ferry.

Twenty minutes later, the ferry whistle blew and the craft left the dock. As it churned across the water, Kemper and Achebe stood at the rail. The day was overcast, threatening rain. First they watched the harbor disappear behind them. Then they watched the sea in silence. No one brought them any food as midday came and went, which made Kemper believe their next contact was not on board, but waiting for them at the ferry's destination.

"Do you now think the cautious faction was right?" Achebe asked him quietly. "That we should have waited to send the *Doncella* to Kyra-2B?"

"No," said Kemper. "I think we should have gone when we did. There were pressing concerns."

"So there were. Overpopulation, for one."

"Yes. The mission unified us, as a race. Gave us something to rally behind."

"I remember." Achebe's tone was wistful.

"Which faction do you believe was right?" Kemper asked.

"None of them," said Achebe. "I think, perhaps, we should not have gone at all."

"One thing is certain," Kemper reminded him, "If we hadn't gone on the mission, we'd be long in the ground by now."

Achebe didn't reply to that.

Eventually, in early afternoon, they spotted a sliver

of land to the west. It grew larger until another harbor drew near and the ferry docked.

Kemper and Achebe waited until most of the people had shuffled off the ferry. When no one approached them, Kemper glanced at Achebe. The pilot shrugged. Kemper shrugged back, and the two of them joined the flow of debarking passengers, trailing the bulk of the group.

At the dock, they were met by a man in a military uniform. He appeared to be in his fifties and was flanked by a pair of much younger soldiers carrying rifles.

"Adrian Kemper?" the man asked, though he pronounced the name in an odd cadence and with the emphasis misplaced.

"Yes," Kemper answered. He motioned to Achebe. "Lethabo Achebe."

The military man's eyes flicked to Achebe. He noted the pilot's wound without reaction, then his gaze went back to Kemper. "Come," he ordered, though to Kemper's ear, it sounded more like *koom*.

Flanked by the two armed soldiers, Kemper followed the uniformed man away from the dock. After a short distance, they reached a vehicle with another soldier standing by the driver's door. The vehicle was topless, and the back section had two short benches on each side, room enough for four men, six if they squeezed in tightly.

The leader didn't look back, only settled into the front passenger seat. One of the guarding soldiers motioned for Kemper and Achebe to get in back. He watched as Kemper climbed inside, then held out his hand for Achebe. With a grunt, Achebe heaved himself upward. Kemper saw the pilot wince before he sat down next to him. Both guards clambered inside and dropped on the bench across from them. One shouldered his rifle. The other planted the butt end on the floor of the vehicle and watched Kemper and Achebe with a stony expression.

"I'm still not sure if this is a rescue or prisoner transfer," Kemper murmured.

Next to him, Achebe made an indistinct sound.

The driver started the vehicle and drove.

The trip through the town was quick. It appeared to be slightly smaller than the one they'd recently left, but every bit as developed. Kemper wondered at the difference between these two settlements and the one where Kapitajn had docked, which struck him as more of a hamlet. Soon, though, they were out of the town and his questions faded as they sped down a paved roadway through open country. The wind whipped around them and a rushing noise filled Kemper's ears. The sound reminded him of the battered *Doncellita* filling with water once he and Achebe had splashed down in the sea.

He had expected their destination to be London. His curiosity about what had been a massive metropolis in his own time grew as they sped down the roadway. He guessed the trip would take a couple of hours. Thus, he was surprised when the vehicle slowed and took a turn off the main thoroughfare after less than half that. The new road was also paved but slower going due to more turns.

After another twenty minutes, they arrived at a gate

to a base. The vehicle stopped briefly, but was quickly waved through once the man in the passenger seat identified himself. The driver took them through the streets of the base at a much slower speed, eventually stopping in front of a building.

Kemper tried to make sense of the sign in front. While many of the letters were recognizable, the word itself was not.

The leader exited the car and gestured for them to follow. Kemper and Achebe obeyed. The two armed soldiers trailed behind.

Inside, the man identified himself to a sentry, then led the group down a long hallway, turned right and went part way down another long hallway. He stopped at a door and held it open for them. Kemper and Achebe entered, but their guards did not. The military man held up his hand and said, *"Woat."*

Kemper nodded. "We'll wait," he affirmed.

The man pulled the door shut. Kemper heard a key in the lock.

He glanced at Achebe, who radiated back his usual stoicism.

The room consisted of a few chairs and a low table. A pitcher of water and several glasses sat on the table. Kemper helped himself, pouring one for his pilot as well.

Their "woat" was barely more than ten minutes. The lock rattled and the door opened. A man in his late sixties entered. His light gray hair had thin streaks of white in it. He wore a dark blue garment of a design that looked to be a cross between a lab coat and a nurse's smock. The bottom hem hung just above his knees. In his hands, the man carried only a pen and notepad.

Deep wrinkles creased the man's craggy face, but his eyes were bright and intelligent. Kemper thought he detected kindness there, as well, which was only reinforced when the man smiled at them.

Then he said, "Hello. My name is Ankeny. Welcome home, gentlemans."

16

At first, the clear, if stilted, English surprised Kemper.

Then he noted the slight error in the use of the plural.

That didn't stop him from smiling. "You speak English," he said.

Ankeny bobbed his head several times. "I have to studied Late English for much years. It was necessary for my research."

"Research?"

"I am a military historian." He gestured toward the furniture. "Shall we to sit? I have asked the surjent to bring food."

Kemper took one of the chairs while Achebe settled into the other. As he watched Ankeny sit down in the remaining chair, Kemper glanced at Achebe. The pilot gave him a solemn nod, which he took to mean *lead the way.*

"We have a lot of questions," Kemper said, turning to Ankeny.

"I am certain you do." The historian crossed one leg

over the other and folded his hands. "I will do my best to answer those questions, of course. First, I must to know—are you telling the truth about being astronauts?"

"Yes. Why would we lie about that?"

"There are many reasons men to lie."

"Our ship fell from the sky."

"The Danslander constable said you were rescued in a raft at sea by a fishing trawler."

"After we crash landed," said Kemper.

Ankeny pressed his lips together. "The soldiers here are quite adept at interrogation, I must to warn you."

"There is no need to interrogate us," Kemper replied evenly. "We will answer any question freely. I don't know exactly what we are now, but when we left this planet, all of the crew were members of the World Defense Federation, assigned to the Central Space Administration."

Ankeny's eyes lit up at Kemper's words. "I believe your claim, sirs. No spy would to make that claim. And you should know, my assessment will carry many weight with the commander. I must be able to validate your account."

"Validate how?"

"Through our discussion, for first. Also, I will to verify details where records exist. It is unfortunate your people did not to write in stone nearly as much as the distant ancients did."

Kemper blinked. "You keep doing that."

"Doing what, sirs?"

"Using the infinitive of the verb when you don't need it. I will *to* verify. Did not *to* write." Kemper shook his head. "Will verify. Did not write."

"Ah." Ankeny elongated the word, nodding his head in understanding. He reached for the notepad on the table and scribbled rapidly. "It is sometimes confusing."

"It was for non-native speakers in our own time, as well."

"Please, sirs, if I to make..." He paused, smiling slightly. Then he spoke deliberately. "If I make other errors, will you tell me?"

"Of course."

Ankeny finished his note, then looked up. "My orders are debrief you. We may—"

"You actually do use the infinitive there," Kemper corrected. "Your orders are *to* debrief us."

"Of course," Ankeny said. "*To* debrief you. But the task itself is left for me... *to* decide how is best."

Kemper nodded, both at the message and the grammar.

Ankeny continued. "If I doubted your truth, I would require your account first. I am comfortable you intend to tell me all."

"We will," Kemper agreed, and next to him, Achebe nodded.

"Then," said Ankeny, "we should attend to your physical needs. I see you have found the water. Food is on the way." He glanced at Achebe. "He appears to be injured. Does the wound require treatment?"

Kemper remained silent so Achebe could answer for himself.

"I believe I'm fine for the moment," the pilot said. "Perhaps later, a doctor could take a look."

"Certainly," Ankeny said. He glanced at Achebe again, then back to Kemper "While we wait for refreshments, I am authorized to answer any of your questions now."

"We would very much like that," said Kemper.

Ankeny put down his notepad and folded his hands again. "What do you wish to know first?"

Kemper turned to Achebe. "Pilot's discretion," he said.

Achebe cleared his throat. "How about an easy one? What year is it?"

Ankeny listened to Achebe, his expression neutral. Then he turned to Kemper. "Is this where you wish to begin?"

Kemper's eyes narrowed. "Yes. That's why my pilot asked the question."

"Very well. We are—"

"Wait." Kemper held up a hand. "We've been dealing with this since we arrived."

"Dealing with what?"

"The ugly looks. Suspicion. The purposeful dismissal or outright shunning of Achebe." He pointed to Achebe's midsection. "Someone stabbed him on the goddamn train. What is the issue everyone takes with him?"

"I think that will be made clear as we exchange information, sir. Please to be..." He paused and corrected himself. "Please be patient."

Kemper stared at Ankeny for a few moments, then turned his gaze to Achebe. The pilot gave him a nod. Kemper thought he could read emotion brewing in the man's eyes, but whether it was hurt, confusion, anger, or all three, he couldn't be certain.

He turned back to Ankeny. "The year?"

"Of course. We are currently in the year twelve hundred and four."

Kemper cocked his head. For a brief moment, he wondered again if they had somehow traveled backward in time, though he knew how ridiculous that thought was. At least, he would have called it ridiculous before experiencing the bending of time he'd gone through on this mission.

"What calendar?" he asked.

"We use only one calendar," said Ankeny. "It begins immediately after Arika."

"Arika? Who is that?"

"Not who, sir. What." It was Ankeny's turn to put up a hand. "Let me explain in a more orderly fashion. What year did you launch your mission?"

Kemper told him.

Ankeny eyes went to the ceiling while he calculated. When he returned them to Kemper, he said, "If I understand the ancient calendar correctly, then I believe that was thirteen hundred ninety-six years ago."

"That's right."

Ankeny's brow knitted. "How is possible? Your people's lifespan—"

"We expected this," Kemper said. "Time dilation. It was part of the mission."

"Time...dilation?"

"Much less time passed for us as the travelers," Kemper said. "Due to our speed."

Ankeny blinked in confusion. "Time passed... differently?"

"Don't dwell on it too much," said Kemper. "The point is, we knew all that time would pass here on Earth while we were gone. What we didn't expect was... the way things are. What happened?"

"It must be quite the shock," Ankeny agreed. "Though I can assure you the Arika was an even greater shock to your people."

"That's the second time you've said *your* people," Kemper said. "Aren't you *our people*?"

"Oh, no." Ankeny shook his head. "I am afraid not."

"In our day—"

"All the people of the world were one?" Ankeny asked, raising a brow.

"Well, yes."

Ankeny leaned forward earnestly. "Was that truly so?"

Kemper nodded. "It wasn't absolute. Human nature is flawed. But for the overwhelming majority, yes."

"How did that work?" the historian asked.

"Work?" Kemper replied. "It didn't work. It simply *was.* We realized we were all one people—the human race."

"No countries?" Ankeny scratched a note on his pad.

"Countries existed," Kemper admitted, "but borders were open and unguarded. Freedom of movement was a basic guarantee."

"And what of race? Religion? Other dogmatic

beliefs? These have been the cause of many wars. We see minor conflicts surrounding them almost every year."

Kemper struggled to understand Ankeny's perception. Finally, he shrugged. "We all knew our own history. Wars over whose god was right. Wars of conquest. Centuries of slavery, of subjugation based upon race, ethnicity, or other differences. But the mindsets that fueled those behaviors were historical, not modern. We looked at them the same way you might look at someone who believes the sun orbits a flat Earth."

"Fascinating." Ankeny spoke the word in a slow and breathy exhale. His eyes were alight with excitement. "This is wonderful information. There is considerable debate amongst the few scholars who study that period. Some feel the level of amity and collaboration was only legend, or at least heavily exaggerated. Or, worse yet, mere propaganda."

"Do you think we could have gone to the stars unless it were true?" Achebe interjected.

Ankeny's gaze flicked to the pilot. A trace of a smile appeared on his lips. "That is the argument the other side makes. It is the side I tend to agree with. Of course, there are also many who deny space travel ever occurred."

"Never occurred?" Kemper choked out the words, surprised.

"The records from that era have been neglected, and are incomplete," explained Ankeny. "There are too many references to space travel for anyone to ignore the topic, but many dismiss it as mythology or intentional fiction, meant as entertainment."

"We flew over three hundred light years and back,"

Kemper said.

"I believe you. But there is no evidence to support your claim."

Kemper opened his mouth to argue, then stopped. The *Doncella* was destroyed, burned up upon re-entry. Had any pieces survived to strike the Earth? Even if they had, would they be distinguishable? What about the *Doncellita?* The shuttle that saved them now lay at the bottom of the North Sea. Even if these people wanted to recover it, he suspected they lacked the technology to do so.

What did that leave? A rubber life raft adrift somewhere on the North Sea, and the two of them. Kemper seized upon the latter, and insisted, "*We* are your evidence."

Ankeny fixed him with a genuinely sad expression but said nothing.

Before Kemper could continue, Achebe gestured between the three of them. "Please, tell me—are you saying we are not all of a people?"

Ankeny's sadness deepened, though a hint of a bittersweet smile touched the corners of his mouth. "Alas, no."

Achebe frowned but said nothing further.

The three men sat in silence for several moments. Then, Kemper asked, "What was Arika?"

The shadow of Ankeny's smile faded. "A catastrophe."

He related the history to them.

Approximately eighty years after the *Doncella's* Meitner drive engaged near the orbital distance of Neptune and sent Kemper and his crew hurtling toward Kyra-2B, a previously untracked asteroid approached Earth. Dubbed Arika, scientists quickly determined it was on a collision course. The military scrambled, managing to get enough weaponry into orbit in time to blast Arika into smaller pieces.

"Those pieces fell to Earth," Ankeny told them. "Many were still large enough to cause local devastation where they struck the surface, but none were of sufficient size to bring about damage on a planetary level. Or so your people thought."

That sounded ominous to Kemper. He motioned for Ankeny to continue.

"The fragments of Arika were responsible for a mutation to the DNA of our species," he said. "We do not know how. It is possible the scientists of the time did not know, either. Or perhaps they did. Their knowledge is largely lost to us. Nonetheless, there are theories it was a substance on the asteroid or an element of the rock itself. Much like the intricacies of DNA, the answer is simply gone, if ever there was one."

Kemper stared at him, processing the information. He saw no obvious difference between Ankeny and himself or Achebe. Ankeny appeared as human as either of them. Perhaps the change was hidden somehow by the historian's smock, however.

"What mutation?" he asked, dreading the answer.

"Within a generation of Arika's arrival, human life span was significantly altered."

"Altered? How?"

"It was reduced," said Ankeny. "The average life span of a man today is thirty-eight years. Women tend to live several years longer."

"Thirty-eight?" Kemper sat back, surprised. Then he motioned toward Ankeny. "But you've got to be sixty or so."

Ankeny smiled indulgently. "I am considered an old man, sir, who has lived a fortunate life. The military has provided me with food and safety. My labors are of the mind, which has spared my body much wear and tear. I am not sixty, however. No one has reached that age in a very many centuries. No, I am forty-one years old."

Kemper stared at him, struggling to match his statement to his appearance.

"It is difficult for you, no?" Ankeny asked. "Even without accounting for the oddities of time and perception that accompanies your travels, the two of you are among the oldest mens... *men* on the planet."

Kemper shook his head, as if to clear it. "This... mutation. It struck within a generation?"

"Yes."

"How?"

"Again, we do not know. Many records were destroyed during the warring period that followed. The knowledge passed down was incomplete. Once the mutation was discovered, learned men and women of the last generation began a form of intellectual triage. What they deemed most important was taught to the next generation. Superfluous pursuits were left by the wayside."

"Like space travel," Achebe murmured.

"Just so," agreed Ankeny. "The academics and scientists prioritized those areas of study essential to our survival as a species."

"What about those who were off-world when Arika hit?" Kemper asked.

"Off-world?" Ankeny tilted his head. "Like yourself, you mean?"

"Yes. In our time, there were a few operations within the solar system. Some mining, some scientific. Were those people affected?"

Ankeny frowned in disappointment. "I am sorry. I have no knowledge of the existence of such peoples, much less their fate. Such things have not been our focus."

"It sounds as though your focus was war," Kemper said bluntly. "And war is rarely the answer."

The historian paused before replying. He glanced around, light concern etched on his face.

"Are you worried someone is listening?" Kemper asked him.

Ankeny smiled weakly. "It is a habit, I'm afraid." Then he chuckled self-consciously. "I don't know why I worry. Even if someone were monitoring this conversation, there are perhaps two or three others in this entire nation who could understand our words."

"This nation?" Kemper asked. "You mean England?"

Ankeny shrugged. "We are called Anglicku, but it is analogous to what you might remember as England. We are the whole of the island, from north to south."

Kemper wanted to ask about the Irish isle but there were more pressing questions. "Why were you worried about someone listening to us?"

"Because our own history is not one to necessarily be prideful about," said Ankeny. "By the time the first generation after Arika was coming into power, the priorities shifted. What was deemed critical survival knowledge was no longer crafts, industries, and farming. Survival became about weaponry. Despite the urgings of the last generation, this was the direction the new generation took. It sowed the seeds of the warring period. It was a war that lasted centuries. A dozen generations."

There was a sharp knock on the door, causing Kemper to start. Ankeny was unperturbed however. He called out, speaking in the same language the military leader had used earlier. The door swung open and a soldier entered with a cart. Wordlessly, he rolled the cart closer and transferred plates of bread, cheese, and a processed meat onto the table between the three men. When he'd finished, he asked Ankeny a question.

The historian shook his head. *"Teeyank ooh, Surjent,"* he said.

The soldier nodded respectfully and left the room.

Ankeny swept a hand toward the food. "Shall we eat?"

"Only if we can talk while we do," said Kemper.

"Of course. I imagine everything I share with you raises new questions."

"It does." Kemper reached for a piece of bread, but didn't take a bite. "Tell me about the mutation."

Ankeny shrugged. "What is to tell? It is no longer a

mutation, is it? After almost fourteen centuries, it is simply life."

"An average life-span of thirty-eight for men?" Kemper asked. "That's only twenty years of adulthood."

"Ah," said Ankeny. "I see your confusion." He took some bread himself, then added meat and cheese to it. He stared down at the food, thinking. "The mutation didn't simply lop off years of life expectancy. More accurately, it compressed our life span." He pressed down on the top piece of bread, flattening it. Then he lifted the thin sandwich and showed it to them. "It is the same, no? Just compressed. We are very similar. Puberty occurs around age seven. Physical maturity at eleven or twelve. Here in our nation, compulsory military service occurs in our thirteenth year."

Kemper sat holding his crust of bread, letting the concept seep in. "Compressed," he murmured, as if saying the word would help him process the idea.

"Just so," said Ankeny, and bit into his flattened sandwich.

17

Kemper changed his mind about talking during lunch. Instead, the three men ate in silence, each alone with his thoughts.

At first, Kemper was struck by the parallel to what he and his crew discovered on Kyra-2B. The devolution of a civilization. For the Kyrans, the fall seemed almost complete. Here on Earth, it was only marginally less pronounced. He contemplated the fallout of such a cataclysmic change. Slowly, the archaic technology he and Achebe saw from the time they were pulled aboard the fishing trawler to this moment made much more sense. A picture began to form of a world-wide society dissolving back into nations, of nations warring, and isolationism. In his time, those traits and behaviors were in the past; though, not so distant that the lessons learned by them enabled humans to resist those compulsions in the present. However, if those hard lessons were forgotten, he was confident human nature was such that the mistakes would be repeated with enthusiasm.

Ankeny confirmed as much once their lunch was

finished. "The last generation was wise enough to immobilize the largest threats before the shift completely occurred," he said. "Nuclear weaponry, nuclear power, and other weapons of mass destruction were themselves destroyed. The knowledge of their creation and operation was not shared and it is now gone to us. It is the only lost information historians like myself are grateful to be rid of. Given the ferocity and length of the warring period, if our people were capable of that level of destruction, they would have certainly used it." He smiled wanly. "You would have returned to a wasteland, sir, instead of merely to a world that has moved on."

"Moved on?" Kemper said. "That is a poetic way to put it."

Ankeny shrugged. "I borrowed it from a piece of ancient literature. But it is fitting."

"These wars," Kemper asked. "Who fought them?"

"Everyone," Ankeny said simply. "It is said they occurred in almost every region of the world, especially once the last generation had passed away. Nations formed along ethnic lines. There were a few grand alliances, such as the powers that aligned against the Rus." He shook his head. "That was our greatest struggle, here in what you once called Europe. The Rus expanded westward. The northern peoples banded with the Germanic to slow their advance. We joined the war, along with those in the southwest. *Le Frankelen*, you know?"

"The French?"

Ankeny turned up his hands. "The descendants of the same, yes. Together, the Four Peoples fought the

Rus. The battle lines shifted east to west and back again. The war raged for many generations. I imagine, eventually, many soldiers did not even know why they were even fighting. It would not surprise me if many of the Rus tell a different tale of this era—how the alliance of western aggressors invaded their nation, and so forth. After Arika, much was forgotten, easily and quickly. Perhaps even willingly. But not grudges. No, those we clung to as if our survival depended on it. Ironic, when you realize those grudges did more to endanger our survival than protect us."

"Your people have moved beyond the warring period now?"

Ankeny shrugged. "The worst of it ended hundreds of years ago. Lines were drawn that have remained largely intact. The wars heavily damaged our infrastructure, so people were forced to turn their focus inward. Recover what knowledge we could so we were able to concentrate on those matters that truly did contribute to our survival. As a result, our technology stagnated and regressed. We discovered many ancient ways that still worked. For example, you rode from Dansland on a train, did you not?"

Kemper nodded. "Coal-powered?"

"Just so. Steam is another common source of energy."

"We rode here in a military vehicle," Kemper pointed out.

"Yes. Petroleum-based fuel is restricted here to military use only. Even in other nations who have no such restriction, only the wealthiest citizens can afford to access it." Ankeny rose and refilled his water glass at the nearby table. When he returned, he held the pitcher over Kemper's glass, which was half-full. Kemper nodded his thanks and Ankeny filled it. The historian hesitated, then repeated the process with Achebe. As the water filled the pilot's glass, Ankeny said to him, "I should explain the... attitude you've experienced, sir."

"I believe I understand," Achebe said. "The world must have become a much smaller place after the mutation."

"It did," said Ankeny. "After the devastation of the warring periods between nations, people withdrew into their own small regions, then further withdrew into their towns and cities. Over centuries, a distrust of outsiders is become embedded in every local psyche."

"Became," corrected Kemper absently, soaking in the bleak picture painted by the historian.

"Ah, thank you," Ankeny replied. "Anyhow, at a national level, hatreds lived on. The Four Peoples and the Rus do not trade. We do not even much communicate. Enmity remains from generation to generation. It is that enmity, I believe, the only thing that keeps the Four Peoples' fragile alliance stitched together." He motioned toward Achebe. "Your treatment is a result of that clannish mentality, and the lingering effects of several wars *Le Frankelen* fought with the dark-skinned peoples. If you had not been with your companion, such treatment may have been more frequent and even harsher than the singular attack you experienced."

"My savior," Achebe intoned, his voice laced with

both humor and rancor.

"If you had you landed off what you would call the African coast, your roles would have been very much reversed, I assure you." Ankeny paused, then shrugged. "Or so I have been told. Our interaction outside of our own nation is mostly limited to the other three Peoples."

"Technological limitations?" Kemper inquired.

"Partially but mostly social ones. Our focus remains very internal, both as a society and as individuals."

"What do you mean?"

"Each nation is concerned mostly with the affairs within its borders. There are some few key resources that are traded but, other than that, we tends to pay attention to our own lands rather than any others."

"Isolationism," said Kemper.

"Just so," Ankeny agreed. "This trend, it is also cultural. One of the results of a shortened life span has been that many of our citizens embrace a modified sort of hedonism. Time is not to be wasted, or even spent in vast quantities, on anything that does not bring pleasure or serve an immediate purpose."

"You mean like learning an ancient language?"

Ankeny smiled broadly, the lines of his face stretching when he did so. "I am an anomaly, sir. Most would surmise I have wasted my life with my pursuits."

"Maybe our return will change that."

Ankeny's smile faded slightly. "It is good for you I am here, I believe. This conversation validates my life's work. Sadly, I don't think your arrival will impact anyone outside of this room. No one will much care. I am sorry."

"The world has moved on." Kemper repeated

Ankeny's earlier phrase.

"Just so. Even the military views my studies as having questionable value. Each subsequent generation seems to embrace that belief more completely."

Kemper thought back to his own days as a student, learning the history of the world, including the British Isles. "It was like that here once before," he said. "After the Romans left Britain. There was a collapse of sorts. A loss of knowledge across the spectrum of society."

"The Romans," mused Ankeny. "Our understanding of the deep ancients is fragmentary, though their monuments have tended to be more illuminating than those relics from your time, sir."

"We relied primarily on digital methods."

"The invisible world," lamented Ankeny. "Another lost technology. The means to read these texts lasted for a generation or two after Arika, but the infrastructure failed early in the warring period. Once the immediate practical use was not possible, the resources needed to sustain the technology were deemed... superfluous. And ultimately forgotten."

"You were talking about culture earlier?" Kemper prodded.

"Ah, yes. I was pointing out that the temperament for long studies exists only rarely these days. There are a few of us who pursue one or perhaps two areas of scholarship. We keep the knowledge alive for the next generation if any care to follow."

"What do people do instead?"

"Some serve. Most simply live. Our world is still frequently marred by small wars. Border skirmishes, mostly. Day to day, the infrastructure is supported where it serves our needs but there is little growth, if any. Maintenance is key. We are fortunate here. In some places, even that process is a losing battle."

Kemper took in the information, mulling it over. He felt numb from the enormity of what Ankeny had shared, and his mind was roiling with more questions. Dozens of them. Hundreds. He was beginning to realize he would have plenty of time to discover those answers. There was one question more pressing than the rest, though.

"Is there any remnant of the WDF remaining?" he asked. "Or the CSA?"

Ankeny shook his head. "Alas, no."

"Then we are no longer in any service," Kemper said.

"I think not," Ankeny agreed.

"Are we prisoners here?"

"No. But your movement will be restricted, at least until our debrief is complete."

"What about the trusts created for us?"

"Trusts?"

"Money, set aside for our return."

"Ah, I see." Ankeny said. "Gone, I'm afraid. Erased, centuries past."

Kemper looked over at Achebe. "So much for your wealth, my friend."

"Freedom and family are the greatest riches," Achebe told him. "I value those more than any amount of money."

"I can't speak for family," said Ankeny, "but there is another consideration." Ankeny's gaze flicked to Achebe and back to Kemper. "For both of you."

"What is that?"

Ankeny again glanced around, as if concerned about eavesdropping. Carefully, he said, "Your DNA pre-dates Arika. Thus, your lifespan has not been compressed. If you father children, those traits will be passed on to them."

"Aren't the effects of Arika still present?" Kemper asked.

"We do not know what caused the mutation," Ankeny said. "We do not know if it is still at work. We do know our population struggles to grow. In some places, it is decreasing. If you were able to inject the trait of your lifespan into the gene pool, it might make a difference."

Kemper shook his head at the irony. "In our time, the problem was too many people. Now, the problem is too few?"

"Just so."

"It makes one wonder," he mused. "Perhaps the arrival of Arika was simply nature's way of stepping in and solving the overpopulation problem."

"That is hardly a scientific view," said Ankeny. "It presupposes design, does it not?"

Kemper shrugged. "Much of nature indicates design, even if it is only the outcome of millennia of evolution."

"I am only an historian," Ankeny said. "My focus is on the past. The military's focus is on the present, and the future. Reintroducing your genetic traits into the population might very well influence both."

"We'd be mating with women who have the mutated gene," said Achebe. "I'm no microbiologist, but that mitigates the odds of passing on the correct genes. I suspect any impact on the larger population would be minimal."

"Nonetheless, is it not your duty?" Ankeny tilted his head as he spoke. "As a patriotic human?"

Achebe glanced at Kemper, who returned his gaze stoically. Kemper wondered if Achebe's thoughts mirrored his own. *Was* it a duty? Could he ever love another, after Holly? What if the military forced the matter? Would he spend the rest of his life on this base, compelled to impregnate their chosen surrogates?

Achebe turned back to Ankeny. "Even if we were to agree with your premise, there is the matter of stellar infertility."

Ankeny's brow scrunched. "Pardon?"

"The effects of space travel runs the extraordinarily high risk of rendering both men and women infertile. Gravitational fluctuations, radiation... not to mention exposure to an alien planet." He shrugged. "We'd have a ten percent chance, at best. Even if we were successful, the resulting offspring might have significant abnormalities."

Ankeny appeared crestfallen. "That is... disappointing."

Not as disappointing as the prospect of being held captive as a prized stud, Kemper thought.

Ankeny considered the news for a long while before he spoke again. "My superiors have not yet considered the possibility of what you could provide in genetic terms.

Clearly, the prospect of increased lifespan will be attractive to them. It would serve to increase the size of our standing army, for one thing."

"Too bad we are both infertile," said Kemper, his tone deliberate.

"Yes," Ankeny said, nodding slowly, his eyes alight with understanding. "It is unfortunate. Even if you were not, I am certain the lingering effects of Arika would only render any results moot after another generation."

"A tragedy," intoned Achebe.

The trio remained silent for a few moments. Then Ankeny cleared his throat. "My report will be clear on this point, sirs. As such, I believe you should consider yourselves free men. Or you will be, once our debriefing is complete."

"Then perhaps we should get on with that," Kemper suggested.

"Very well." Ankeny sounded eager as he reached for his notepad. "Let us begin."

Kemper motioned for Achebe to speak first. The pilot described their mission, the personnel, and their initial journey. Ankeny marveled at the technology Achebe described, but did not ask the man to explain it further. Instead, he scribbled notes furiously, sometimes asking the pilot to pause while he caught up.

Achebe spoke until he had reached the point in the story in which the crew took the *Doncellita* to the planet's surface. Kemper picked up the tale from there, recounting their exploration, the contact with the tall

Kyrans—

Elves, Shu called them. And Orcs were the fierce ones.

—and the subsequent attacks. He tried to gloss over the decisions he had to make the morning after Worona was wounded, but Ankeny was meticulous in his questions. He explored the entire scenario in great detail. By the time Kemper finished relating it, his throat was dry and his voice strained with weariness.

Achebe resumed the account. He told Ankeny of their trip home, the failure of Shu's cryo pod, and the difficult nature of their descent into the sea.

"I believe you know the rest," the pilot said, his resonant baritone perfect for storytelling. "Our rescue and subsequent trip to your nation?"

"Yes," said Ankeny. "When necessary, our communication with the other three Peoples is quite efficient. Those messages were vague, however. I did not know whether to expect insane men or ones who were truly astronauts."

"Now you know," said Achebe.

"Unless you don't believe us," Kemper added, surprised at how tired he sounded even to his own ear.

"I am quite certain you are being truthful," Ankeny assured them. "As I mentioned, my opinion will greatly influence the commander's view."

"Why does his view matter?" asked Kemper. "If we are free men?"

"If you were insane, or agents of the Rus, you would not be free. I will assure him you are neither."

"What will become of us, then?"

"It will be as I said. You will be free men." His gaze flicked to Achebe. "With my apologies, sir, your freedom will come with a caveat."

"Let me guess," said Achebe. "I am to leave your lands."

Ankeny nodded. He did not seem embarrassed, but his expression bore the hint of regret, or sympathy. Kemper could not tell which.

"It is well," Achebe responded. "I will return to my home. There will be family for me there."

"I sincerely hope so," Ankeny said. "In any event, we will help you arrange transportation."

Achebe dipped his chin in thanks.

Ankeny turned to Kemper. "And you, sir? What will you do?"

"Maybe I should become a history teacher," Kemper mused.

Ankeny laughed heartily. When he had finished, he said, "Your wit is singular, sir. Though your jest is not entirely implausible. Your historical knowledge would be an incredible asset."

"To whom?"

"Whomever you should choose. I suspect you would be welcome anywhere amongst the Four Peoples. The military would gladly employ you. Or a learning institution, such as they are."

"From captain to professor," said Kemper.

"Just so. Where should you like to go?"

Kemper rubbed his chin thoughtfully. "In our time, there was an island to the northwest called Ireland?"

"Yes. The island is still there, of course, though it

has another name now. The whole island is its own nation but we remain on cordial terms." Ankeny cocked his head. "Why do you ask?"

Kemper smiled then, perhaps his first of this long day.

"I once had a house," he said.

18

The full debrief went on for nearly a month.

Ankeny's superiors seemed satisfied with his assessments, at least according to the historian. He reviewed their accounts with them multiple times, filling out smaller and smaller details each time. After the first day, he began interviewing the two men separately. Had Ankeny begun their interactions that way, this might have concerned Kemper. It was a classic interrogation tactic. But he'd come to trust the historian, particularly after his reaction to their discussion of the men's genetic responsibility.

They were given clothing that consisted of military utility trousers and the issued undershirt. Modest quarters were also provided—a small room with a pair of cots, essentially. A washroom facility was down the hall. When not in conversation with Ankeny, the pair was restricted to this area. Meals were initially brought to them, and that trend continued unless their interview schedule intersected with chow times. Eventually, however, their guards escorted them to the dining hall and they sat at the same long tables as the other soldiers.

The soldiers stared at first. A few muttered in dark tones. After a week, their presence became less of a novelty and they were mostly ignored. The spaces on the benches near them were left empty, creating an invisible buffer no one seemed willing to cross. The few times the dining hall was overfull, several soldiers remained standing until seating opened up elsewhere rather than sit next to the strangers.

Kemper used the time to read. Or tried to, anyway. Ankeny loaned him a copy of what he called an ancient book—what Kemper would have labeled a classic: *The Old Man and the Sea by Ernest Hemingway*. The tome was hardcover, and hundreds of years old, at least. It was a translation into Anglicku, a trend Ankeny told him was becoming uncommon. The pages were brittle and the corners of several broke off in Kemper's fingers as he read.

He knew the original book well. He'd read it several times, most recently while sitting in the living room of his beloved house. The fact this had technically occurred almost fourteen hundred years ago weighed on him as he struggled with the words that seemed both foreign and familiar at the same time. The hopeful focus of the protagonist in the novel as he fished for, and finally caught, a large marlin helped buoy his mood, though the novel's eventual outcome tempered that.

When he'd worn himself out on Hemingway, he turned to the language primers Ankeny gave them both to study. While the exercises within were designed for children, Kemper still found them difficult. But phrase by phrase, word by word, he built a small linguistic toolbelt for himself. No doubt he sounded like an illiterate tourist with a horrific accent, but at least he could ask and answer a few basic, essential questions in the tongue of the Anglicku. While those on the island he knew as Ireland spoke a different tongue, he was assured many there would at least understand him when he spoke his newly-learned phrases.

Achebe spent much of his time reading as well, though Ankeny was unable to secure any textbooks in the languages spoken in Western Africa. Still, the pilot applied himself diligently to learning Anglicku.

The knife wound Achebe received on the train healed slowly and no infection set in. From what Kemper could tell, the medical capabilities of the military on the base were akin to that of the early-to-mid Twentieth Century. Depending on the ailment, he felt like surviving treatment would be hit-or-miss.

Finally, their debrief came to an end. Ankeny expressed genuine sadness their time together was over.

"I have learned more in the past month than in all my years of study," he told them. "You have engendered in me a far greater admiration for our ancestors. Thank you."

Kemper thanked him for advocating for them, for skirting the issue of their fertility, and for making arrangements for their journeys to come. Ankeny had made all of the necessary phone calls and even secured a small sum of travel money for each of them.

"It was not difficult," the historian assured him. "We are a civilized people."

That night, as they lay in their cots, Kemper and Achebe found themselves talking about the crew of the *Doncella.* They reminisced in low, soft voices, reminding each other of as many moments and trivial details about each of their comrades, as if trying to ensure the maximum amount of knowledge was cemented within the minds of both of them.

"Kyra-2B," Kemper murmured. "Seven hundred years ago, we were on its surface. Grussmacher and Worona—do you think they survived?"

"I like to think there's a tribe of humans ten or twelve generations on living there now," said Achebe. "A family that is both theirs and somehow ours, as well."

"That's a nice sentiment," Kemper said wistfully.

"It is."

Kemper thought of the Hemingway novel and of the marlin Santiago tried to haul to shore after he'd caught it. Achebe's optimistic scenario reminded him of the fisherman's hope. A hope that the sharks soon dashed.

The two men slept, but Kemper imagined they had very different dreams.

In the morning, they said their goodbyes.

Bidding farewell to Ankeny proved harder than Kemper expected. The historian was intelligent, inquisitive, and kind. He had been the gateway to most of Kemper's knowledge about this new world in which he now lived. When they clasped hands, Ankeny dropped his other hand over the top and squeezed hard.

"I wish you good fortune, sir," he said to Kemper,

his voice laced with emotion.

"And you."

Ankeny paused, before adding, "Should you ever choose to have a family, I wish your children a long and prosperous life."

Kemper smiled slightly. "You are very kind."

Ankeny turned to Achebe without any of the hesitation he'd shown in their first meeting. He held out his hand and Achebe took it.

"I wish you good fortune as well, my friend," he said.

"Thank you," Achebe replied. "May your remaining days be pleasant."

"The revelations you've shared will help make them so," Ankeny assured them.

The historian walked them to the front of the building, where he left them. The only possession Kemper held was the battered Hemingway book Ankeny had insisted on making a gift to him. Kemper and Achebe stood waiting for the soldiers who would drive them to their separate destinations. Achebe was bound for London, where he would take a ship and sail south to his homeland. Kemper was going by car to the northwest coast, where he would also board a ship, but for a much shorter journey.

"This is nothing like what I imagined it would be," Achebe said quietly.

"No," Kemper agreed. "It is not."

"We are alive, Captain. We have that, at least."

"We do."

A vehicle pulled up to them. The driver, a scowling soldier with thick, bristly hair, motioned for Achebe to get in. The pilot turned toward Kemper and raised his hand in a slow salute. Kemper returned the gesture.

"It has truly been an honor," Achebe said.

"The honor is mine," Kemper replied. "Without you, our mission would have failed."

Achebe smiled sadly. "We did fail, Captain. But we are both alive because of you."

Kemper didn't argue the point, though their survival had hinged just as much on Achebe's actions throughout the mission as his own. Instead, he nodded appreciatively.

The soldier behind the driver's wheel barked out an impatient order. Achebe held out his hand toward Kemper. Kemper reached out to take it, but stopped. A thought that he'd been having over the past month—that Achebe was the only, and last, person alive from his own time suddenly weighed on him. Without thinking, he stepped forward and drew his friend into a tight embrace.

Achebe appeared unsurprised. His sinewy arms squeezed Kemper tightly in return. Kemper wanted to tell the man how much he wished him well, hoped he would find his extended family and be rich in spirit as he'd described before. The words caught in his throat and all he could do was squeeze harder.

For his part, Achebe only turned his head slightly and kissed Kemper on the temple. "Safe journey, my Captain," he murmured. Then the pilot pulled away. When he was at arm's length, he clapped Kemper on both shoulders with his palms, smiled crookedly, and climbed into the military vehicle. The driver goosed the accelerator and sped away.

Kemper watched them go. It was at that moment he felt truly alone for the first time in many centuries.

213

19

His own journey was brief and uneventful.

First, another soldier arrived in a separate vehicle. They left the base and drove for several hours in silence. When they reached a small port town, the soldier contacted another official—perhaps a constable; Kemper couldn't be certain—and handed off his charge. The official brought Kemper to the docks and handed him off to a ship captain.

The small vessel that ferried him across what had once been the Irish Sea was no bigger than the fishing trawler that had rescued them after they crashed the *Doncellita.* The captain, a bearded man with grizzled features, bade Kemper to remain near him in the wheelhouse for the entirety of the trip.

When they docked, it was at an even smaller village than the one from which they'd departed. The captain waved him to go ashore. On the docks, a slender woman waited for him. They spoke haltingly in a combination of what Kemper now thought of as Late English and the language of Anglicku.

The woman introduced herself as Grita.

"You are an historian?" he asked. "Like Ankeny?"

"Not like Ankeny," she said. "Much lesser."

Kemper wondered if she meant she was less accomplished in her field than Ankeny or, if she wasn't a full-time historian, but he didn't feel like their level of shared fluency could handle exploring the matter. Instead, he said, "Thank you for helping me." Then he repeated as much of the phrase as he could in Anglicku.

Grita smiled slightly at his attempt. Graciously, she corrected his word order and pronunciation. Once he'd restated the phrase correctly, she gave him a vigorous nod.

"You fast ear," she said. "Will to be good for learning our language." She waved for him to follow. "Come. We go house."

Kemper followed.

Grita led him into the heart of the village. After a short walk, she stopped at a bicycle rack. She removed one and indicated another Kemper should take. Hesitantly, he did so. "I haven't ridden since I was a child," he said.

Grita cocked her head. "You can no do?"

"I can," he assured her, then repeated it in Anglicku.

Grita grunted her approval. She mounted the bicycle and pedaled west. Kemper swung a leg over his bicycle and quickly followed. After the first few wobbling yards, he found his balance.

Once they were out of the village, he pulled up beside her. "Does someone live in the house now?" he asked.

Grita nodded. "They live there."

"Is it someone from my family?" The hopeful sound ringing in his own voice surprised him. Even at the time the CSA found someone to act as steward for his house, it had been a distant relative. After Arika, he imagined the stewardship disappeared, along with everything else from before.

But Grita only shrugged at his question. Either she did not know or the answer did not matter, Kemper was unsure which.

The countryside looked vaguely familiar in places, though Kemper couldn't be certain if that was his own mind wishing it so. When they reached the tiny hamlet where his house was, the sense of familiarity felt more concrete, though still fleeting.

Grita led him down a narrow road of broken pavement, then turned left. As soon as Kemper swung the bicycle onto the short lane, he saw it.

His house.

Kemper stopped pedaling and coasted slowly towards the dwelling. The stone exterior looked far more battered and worn than he remembered but that was to be expected. The structure remained stout, he thought. Not sagging on its foundation or appearing fragile in any way. The large windows that let the light in had different frames than he remembered; thicker, more functional than aesthetic. But the glass was intact.

"Was your home?" Grita asked.

"Yes," he whispered hoarsely.

They set the bikes against a low stone wall and approached the house.

"Do they know we are coming?" he asked Grita in Anglicku.

She nodded absently and rapped on the door. A man in his late fifties answered. The woman standing at his shoulder looked to be the same age.

Not late fifties, Kemper amended. *Late twenties.*

Grita spoke to the couple briefly. They replied, clearly displeased with the exchange. Grita's tone grew more forceful. Kemper understood none of the words— Grita was clearly speaking in the tongue of this island— but the nature of the discussion was unmistakable.

They were defending their home.

Finally, the man stopped arguing with Grita. The woman said a few more choice words then put her hand on the man's shoulder. He pushed the door open and stood partially aside.

Kemper made no move to enter. "What are you called?" he asked in Anglicku.

The man's scowl deepened.

"The Anglicku is not for good to speak here," Grita told him. "Some bad feelings for my people."

"I'm sorry," said Kemper. "Ankeny said relations between your nations were cordial."

"Ankeny not know all. He spend much his time in the past." She shrugged. "Speak the Late English. I know enough for to translate."

"All right." He glanced at the man in the doorway, who was scowling at the two of them. "Did he understand my question?"

"No," said Grita. "They only know it was Anglicku." She spoke a few words to the couple, clearly translating

Kemper's query.

The man didn't reply, but his wife finally said, "Mara." Then she gestured to her husband and said, "Kivan."

Kemper touched his chest. "Kemper," he said slowly.

The woman nodded but didn't say anything.

Kemper glanced at Grita. "May I go inside?"

"Yes."

Kemper edged his way past Kivan, who didn't move to create more room for his passage. Inside, the house had an earthy scent to it, punctuated by something cooking in the kitchen. He walked slowly down the hall toward the living room. Simple, well-worn furniture adorned the room. Some afternoon light reflected indirectly through the large windows, giving the space a slight golden hue. He tried to imagine—*no, remember*—what it would look like in the morning hours, with the full force of the rising sun filling the room with light.

There was a sound behind him. He glanced over to see Kivan and Mara shadowing him, their gaze intent and suspicious.

He looked away.

Slowly, he wandered through the large room then briefly stopped in the kitchen. Finally, he walked down the short hallway to the bedrooms. He paused outside the master bedroom, suddenly unwilling to enter. It wasn't his room anymore, and entering would feel like an unforgivable violation of privacy. He sensed his entire presence constituted such a violation in the eyes of Kivan and Mara, but going into the room where they slept went too far.

He turned away, walking back into the large living room. Standing near the fireplace, he gazed out the windows at the forest beyond. Memories of a hundred mornings assaulted him. The bittersweet ache of loss tugged at his chest. He'd lost his crew, his people, his world. Now his home, as well. Nothing remained.

Kemper took a step to leave.

And stopped.

Another memory came to him. His hand reached out and found the stone on the mantle that had always been loose. He twisted and pulled at it. With some effort, the stone came free. Kemper shifted it to his other hand and reached for the challenge coin he'd hidden there before leaving for the mission to Kyra-2B. He wondered how weathered it would be or if its long storage beneath the stone would have preserved it.

The space beneath the stone was empty.

His coin was gone.

Kemper sagged a little. Someone must have found it during his long absence. He wondered who it had been. Were they surprised at the find? Did they know what the coin represented? Did they treasure it? Were there others who had discovered it before the person who eventually took it? People who stared down at the strange coin in wonder and then replaced it carefully beneath the rock?

He didn't know, and he decided it didn't matter.

A floorboard at the entryway to the room creaked. He glanced up to see Mara watching him curiously. He turned away and looked down again at the vacant space.

Perhaps he had been foolish to think the coin would remain hidden for all those many years. Somehow he had hoped he would find it undisturbed. That just one thing about the world he left behind would remain unchanged.

Kemper replaced the loose rock. Then he walked past Mara and down the hallway. As he neared the door, he stopped again. He'd come and seen his house. It was the same and it was also different. It remained but was no longer his. A terrible sense of loneliness erupted within him. The ground beneath him felt unsteady.

He didn't want to stay.

He wanted to leave even less.

Grita waited stoically by the door, watching him.

"Tell them *thank you*," he said to her, his voice a ragged whisper.

Grita turned to Mara and Kivan and spoke. Kemper listened carefully to her words, then cleared his throat and tried to repeat the phrase. Mara seemed to appreciate his clumsy effort but Kivan's scowl didn't relent. The old man said something with a near snarl.

"What was that?" Kemper asked Grita.

"He say this is not your house. Is his house."

Kivan spoke again, his words forceful.

"House is his family now for many generation," Grita translated. "He not to know who you be. Maybe you lie about house. Not matter. If house was once yours, is not any longer."

"I know," Kemper said. "The world has moved on."

Grita cocked her head.

Kemper didn't bother to try to repeat it. Instead, he

said, "Tell him I know. It is his house."

Grita translated the sentiment. Kivan's suspicion didn't diminish. He asked a question.

"You say before house was yours," Grita relayed. "You no want?"

Kemper shook his head. "It is their house," he repeated, his voice now resolute.

Grita spoke. Kivan's expression seemed to soften, as did Mara's. The woman said something, which Grita relayed.

"She's asks if you are certain."

"I am." Kemper nodded his head forcefully. He pointed toward them, then twirled his hand at the house that surrounded them, then brought his finger back to them. "Yours," he said in Late English.

Grita murmured the translation. Kivan's scowl disappeared entirely. Mara actually smiled.

"Tell them *thank you* again," Kemper said. "I'm grateful they let me inside to look around."

Grita told them. Kivan nodded but Mara spoke insistently. When she'd finished, Grita shared what she'd said.

"They ask if you have eaten."

"No," said Kemper.

Grita relayed his answer. After the couple spoke again, she turned to him. "They ask you stay for the evening meal. They insist."

Kemper smiled. "Thank you. I am hungry."

Grita gave his answer. Mara's smile broadened. Kivan dipped his chin in approval. They beckoned him in through the kitchen to the small dining room. Being single, Kemper had rarely used the space himself. Sitting down to a roughhewn table in his own house but in a largely unfamiliar room gave him a strange sensation he couldn't pinpoint. He was home but not home. That was the best he could do to understand the emotion.

Mara and Kivan brought food and dishes to the table. Mara scooped a generous portion into a bowl and gave it to Kemper. Then Kivan did the same for Grita. Afterward, the couple served each other. It was a small ritual, but one Kemper immediately liked.

The foursome ate. The dish was a thick, savory stew of some sort, reminding Kemper of lamb. The sauce was just thick enough to use a fork. Compared to the military fare he had been eating for the past month—adequate fare, but uninspired—this homemade stew was a delicacy.

The intermittent silence at the table was punctuated with frequent questions from Kivan or Mara to Kemper. At times, the translation was difficult, even with Grita's presence. As a result, his hosts stuck to simple questions.

Even those caused interesting reactions. When he explained he had been in the service and served in the CSA, they were confused. He tried to explain what it had been but was met with doubtful stares. When he related his mission to Kyra-2B, Grita struggled to translate. Once she seemed to be successful, both Kivan and Mara burst out in laughter.

Kemper smiled at their mirth. "They don't believe me, do they?" he asked Grita.

The translator shook her head. "They think you perhaps to joke? Or you are one who is to write such stories for peoples to read." She struggled for the word, finally settling on, "Not real. Fun story."

"I understand," Kemper said.

"Is true, but?" Grita asked him. "You to fly far in space?"

"It is true."

Grita looked awestruck. "Ankeny say so, but I to think he maybe is to tease me."

"No teasing."

Mara asked Grita a question. From the tone, Kemper believed she wanted to know what the two of them had been discussing. Grita explained.

Mara and Kivan exchanged a glance. *"Spásairnish,"* said Mara, grinning. Kivan swooped his hand through the air, waggling it, and the couple laughed again heartily.

Kemper smiled and ate.

When he'd finished, Mara offered him another serving. Kemper glanced at Grita. "What is the custom? Is it poor form to refuse? Am I expected to refuse? Is food scarce here?"

"The custom is to eat if you are hungry," Grita told him. "Food is not for to waste but is enough here."

Kemper turned back to Mara and smiled his thanks. He held out his dish for a second helping. "It is delicious," he told her, and Grita relayed the compliment.

Mara glanced to the side, embarrassed and waved his comment away. Kemper didn't need Grita's translation to understand the humility of her reply.

He finished his stew, answering several more questions about himself as they ate. When he'd taken the last bite, Mara offered him thirds, but he placed his hand on his stomach and shook his head.

Together, Kivan and Mara cleared the table.

Kemper stood to leave. "Please thank them for the meal," he said.

Grita did so. "They are happy for your visit."

Kemper smiled and nodded at her words. He started for the door, then stopped. A thought had been nibbling at the corners of his mind throughout dinner, and now he decided to pursue it. He had nothing to lose, after all.

"Ask them if they have any children," Kemper instructed Grita.

The woman translated his question.

"No," she told him. "No more. They go away. Make own family."

Kemper nodded slowly, thinking. Finally, he said, "There are three bedrooms. Would they rent one of them to me?"

"I'm sorry?" Grita asked.

He repeated his question, adding he would find a way to earn money. He thought Ankeny's suggestion was a good one. He'd be an historian or perhaps a history professor. He only needed to earn a modest amount to survive. In the meantime, he had the small sum Ankeny had given him.

Grita clarified his intentions before speaking to the couple. Her explanation took a while, but eventually Kivan and Mara seemed to understand. They had a discussion between themselves, and finally nodded to him and replied.

"They say yes," Grita told him. "If you will to pay,

they will to rent a room. If it does not be good, you must to leave when they ask."

"I accept," Kemper said.

He held out his hand to Kivan. The man hesitated, then tentatively reached out and shook it. When he released it, Kemper held it toward Mara. She eyed his proffered hand briefly, then grasped it and gave it a firm shake.

"It is done," Grita said.

Kemper looked around the living room of his house. Outside, the setting sun was now obscured by nearby trees. The dim light that filtered in was still beautiful, he decided.

"I am to leave?" Grita asked. "You stay?"

"If they are fine with it, yes."

Grita consulted the couple again, then told him he could begin his stay that night.

Kemper thanked her. "I will see you again soon, I'm sure." He thought of the help he might need to secure employment, and beyond that, wondered if he might thirst to speak his own tongue with someone.

Grita smiled slightly. "I to like that. I come tomorrow or next day. Find out all is good."

"Thank you."

Grita nodded, then bade them all good night, and left.

Mara showed him to one of the bedrooms. In his time, he'd used the room as a study. Now, it was furnished with a small bed, a dresser, and a single chair.

Kemper put his book on the chair.

When he looked at Mara in the doorway, Kivan had

joined her. He handed her a steaming mug, which she accepted with murmured thanks. Kivan extended another mug toward Kemper. He took it, trying to approximate the words Mara had used to thank him. Kivan chuckled and shook his head. He repeated the word, gesturing between himself and Mara.

Kemper understood—the word she spoke had been a term of endearment. Instead, he made an attempt at the phrase he managed to approximate earlier. Mara nodded her encouragement.

Kivan lifted the mug to chin level, pointed to himself, then Kemper. *"Tapaleat,"* he said.

"Tapaleat," Kemper repeated.

Kivan nodded, then beckoned with his free hand for Kemper to follow.

The threesome walked out into the back yard. When Kemper purchased the home, the yard had been fenced, but once he moved in, he'd removed the fencing. Since then, no one had seen fit to replace it. As a result, there was a clear view of the other homes scattered throughout the hamlet. In the background, an orange-violet band of light from the sunset slashed through the sparse trees. Mara and Kivan stood shoulder-to-shoulder, staring out at the sight.

Kemper took a sip of the tea. It had an earthy taste that left him feeling grounded. He took a deep breath and let it out in a long, slow exhale.

This was no longer his house.

It wasn't his world any longer, either.

Even so, as he watched the light from the sun fade into dusk, Kemper resolved to live in both.

Acknowledgments

I'd like to thank:

Colin Conway, for asking the right questions.

Anne Graham, for putting the story to the eye test from a veteran sci-fi reader.

John Emery, Paula Dunn, Brad Hallock, Beth Camp, Gary Felix, Suzanne Peckham, Ron Sarich, Bill Romaine, Phil Van Itallie, and Susan Bryson for giving the book a first pass, and providing meaningful feedback.

Piers Anthony, whose work fostered my love of fantasy and science fiction, as well as a dream to write both.

Kristi, as always.

About the Author

Frank Saverio has loved science fiction and fantasy since he was young. He was inspired by classics from J.R.R. Tolkien and Phillip K. Dick, as well as later authors such as Piers Anthony, David Eddings, and Lloyd Alexander. More recently, he has enjoyed the work of Joe Abercrombie and George R. R. Martin.

In addition to science fiction and fantasy, Frank writes different genres under different pen names.

As Frank Scalise, he writes mainstream fiction, including middle grade hockey novels and adult drama/comedy (think shades of Jonathan Tropper for the latter).

As Frank Zafiro, he writes gritty crime fiction from both sides of the badge. This includes police procedurals, private investigator novels, and hardboiled. He was a police officer from 1993 to 2013, where he worked patrol, investigations, commanded K9 and SWAT, and retired as a captain.

Frank has written more than 50 novels across all of these genres.

In addition to writing, Frank hosts the podcast *Wrong Place, Write Crime*. He is an avid hockey fan and a tortured guitarist. He lives in Redmond, Oregon.

You can keep up with him at http://franksaverio.net, http://frankscalise.com, and http://frankzafiro.com.

Other Books By Frank Saverio

The Second Degree (A KET novella) (*)

Seasons of Wither Quadrilogy
#1 A Plagued Summer (*)
#2 A Bloody Autumn (*)
#3 A Bleak Winter (*)
#4 A Forgotten Spring (*)

As Frank Zafiro

River City Series
Under a Raging Moon
Heroes Often Fail
Beneath a Weeping Sky
And Every Man Has To Die
The Menace of the Years
Place of Wrath and Tears
Dirty Little Town

Dead Even (short stories)
Some Degree of Murder
No Good Deed (short stories)
The Worst Kind of Truth
Chisolm's Debt
The Cleaner (short stories)
All the Forgotten Yesterdays
Nor Shadowed Heart (*)
Forthcoming River City novel #16 (*)
Forthcoming River City novel #17 (*)
Forthcoming River City novel #18 (*)
The Trade Off
Sugar Got Low (short stories)

Stefan Kopriva Mysteries
#1 Waist Deep
#2 Lovely, Dark and Deep
#3 Friend of the Departed
#4 Hope Dies Last
#5 Think of Laura
#6 The Sins of Somebody Else's Past (*)

SpoCompton Crime Novels
#1 At Their Own Game
#2 In the Cut
#3 All the Pieces Fall
#4 Live and Die This Way
#5 Shades of Knight
#6 All the Minor Kings (*)

<u>Bricks & Cam Jobs</u> (with Eric Beetner)
#1 The Backlist
#2 The Short List
#3 The Getaway List

<u>Charlie-316 series</u> (with Colin Conway)
#1 Charlie-316
#2 Never the Crime
#3 Badge Heavy
#4 Code Four
#5 The Ride-Along
#6 The Silence of the Dead (*)

<u>with Lawrence Kelter</u>
The Last Collar
Fallen City
No Dibs on Murder

<u>The Ania Series</u> (with Jim Wilsky)
#1 Blood on Blood
#2 Queen of Diamonds
#3 Closing the Circle
#0 Harbinger

<u>Jack McCrae Mysteries</u>
#1 At This Point in My Life
#2 All That This Life Requires

<u>Sandy Banks Thrillers</u>
#1 The Last Horseman
#2 Some Kind of Hell
#3 A Hard Favored Death (*)

<u>A Grifter's Song series</u> (creator and editor)
The Concrete Smile (#1)
Come the Apocalypse (#7)
Down Comes the Night (#13)
The Reckoner (#14)
The Alpha Whisperer (#21)
Into the Dying Sun (#35)

As Frank Scalise

All That Counts
A Village of Strangers
A Baker's Divorce
An Unlikely Phoenix
Six Sons (*)
Playing Out the String (*)
Sam the Hockey Player series (middle grade)

(*) forthcoming